# FIT TO BE TIED

The first awareness Gunn had when coming out of sleep was of something warm and soft touching his cheek. There was a muffled giggle. Gunn opened his eyes.

The girl was young, eighteen at most. She was on her knees, straddling his waist. A few of the setting sun's rays found their way into the dark shadows of the tipi and he could see that she was undressed.

"Off, girl," he said.

The girl reached out to touch his lips, then started to unbutton his shirt.

"Off, I said," Gunn grunted. He bent his legs slightly to gain leverage, then arched his back and tried to buck her off. Her hands found his bare flesh and slid over it.

"Untie me," he said.

The girl giggled. Her head dropped to his stomach until desire drove him to oblivion.

When he opened his eyes, he saw the Indian girl slipping her buckskin dress over her head. She came back to him, knelt again and reached out with a hunting knife. She smiled and cut through the strips which held his ankles. He rolled to the right and she freed his hands. By the time he was sitting up she was at the door flap.

"I am Deer Spirit," she said. "Now I have the man-seed which holds the power of Tatanka."

In his pleasure Gunn had concluded that the maiden had been sent to him. Now he wasn't so sure. She had given him a chance to escape from death—and he wasn't going to question why. . . .

# BOLT
## An Adult Western Series by Cort Martin

| | |
|---|---|
| #10: BAWDY HOUSE SHOWDOWN | (1176, $2.25) |
| #11: THE LAST BORDELLO | (1224, $2.25) |
| #12: THE HANGTOWN HARLOTS | (1274, $2.25) |
| #13: MONTANA MISTRESS | (1316, $2.25) |
| #14: VIRGINIA CITY VIRGIN | (1360, $2.25) |
| #15: BORDELLO BACKSHOOTER | (1411, $2.25) |
| #16: HARDCASE HUSSY | (1513, $2.25) |
| #17: LONE-STAR STUD | (1632, $2.25) |
| #18: QUEEN OF HEARTS | (1726, $2.25) |
| #19: PALOMINO STUD | (1815, $2.25) |
| #20: SIX-GUNS AND SILK | (1866, $2.25) |

*Available wherever paperbacks are sold, or order direct from the Publisher. Send cover price plus 50¢ per copy for mailing and handling to Zebra Books, Dept. 1978, 475 Park Avenue South, New York, N.Y. 10016. Residents of New York, New Jersey and Pennsylvania must include sales tax. DO NOT SEND CASH.*

#27

ZEBRA BOOKS
KENSINGTON PUBLISHING CORP.

ZEBRA BOOKS

are published by

Kensington Publishing Corp.
475 Park Avenue South
New York, NY 10016

Copyright © 1987 by Jory Sherman

All rights reserved. No part of this book may be reproduced in any form or by any means without the prior written consent of the Publisher, excepting brief quotes used in reviews.

First printing: January 1987

Printed in the United States of America

*For Sissy*

# Chapter One

The sky was cloudless, the sun at its zenith and the air still as death. A hawk drifted lazily over an outcropping of rocks, its eyes alert for the unwary rabbit or prairie dog, the kangaroo rat, the gray mouse.

Far below the hawk, working his way along a dry creek bed, was a hunter of a different kind. Gunn's trail supplies were gone, but he had too big a hunger for jerky and tinned crackers anyway. He'd been dogging a buffalo track since just after sunup. According to the sign it was a small herd, perhaps no more than a dozen. The big herds ran north in the summer but an occasional rogue and his harem still followed the old trail, along the tributaries of the Missouri.

Gunn was bound for Fort Randall from Fort Robinson. The fort lay at the confluence of the Rosebud and the Missouri. He was carrying a dispatch for Major Waddington. Some of the Crow were up in arms again and there had been a lot of smoke talk about some of them stirring up trouble among the Sioux.

On Gunn's second morning out, while breaking camp, a rattler spooked his pack pony. The pony had a good lead by the time Gunn got saddled up, but he managed to break trail about an hour later. That was too late. A Crow hunting party got there first. There was nothing to do but ride on to Randall, foraging along the way, and until he picked up the buffalo track, the pickings had been slim.

Gunn heard the bellow and so did his mount. Esquire shied a bit but Gunn dismounted and led the horse back down the trail to a bend in the wash. He slipped the Winchester from its saddle sheath and crouched low. He stalked blindly until the wash petered out.

The old rogue bellowed again and Gunn got his first look. He sucked air in through his teeth.

"Well, I'll be damned," he said softly. "Aren't you something?"

The old bull was bigger than most, and he had one horn with a half twist to it. His most astonishing feature however was something else. He was an albino! He was white as a snowdrift with a devil's red tinge in his eyes.

Gunn shifted his weight and cleared away some pebbles so he could dig a solid rest for his left elbow. He hefted the Winchester into position, fitting it snug against his right shoulder, then took aim.

A rabbit scurried from somewhere behind him, darted across his line of sight, then bounded behind a rock. The nearest cow grunted and trotted fifteen or so feet closer to the main herd.

The big white rogue looked up and snorted. Gunn could see the sun sparkle off the saliva stringing from his mouth. He pawed only once, then turned to face Gunn head on.

Gunn waited. A lesser man would have had a

8

difficult time standing patiently in the face of almost a ton of death on the hoof, but using a gun was part of this man's stock in trade. The bull halved the distance, bellowing and snorting. Still Gunn waited.

Gunn knew the old bull would look up just one more time. After that the head would go still lower and that was the moment when Gunn would act. It happened, then, and the Winchester cracked only once.

The bullet cleared the old bull's rock-hard skull and entered the meaty part of his left shoulder, high up. It struck the joint connection and veered downward, imbedding itself into the great beast's heart. The albino's forward momentum carried him only a few more feet. He was dead before his great head struck the dirt.

Gunn watched as the last of the cows rumbled over a grassy knoll and disappeared. He stood and looked toward the buffalo, still now except for the gentle movement of its white fur in the breeze.

Quiet, a stillness found only in that hard and beautiful country, once again settled in. Gunn knelt down, his pale blue eyes almost gray as pewter, and patted the head of the animal. He hated having to kill such a magnificent beast, but at least there would be no waste. He would take what he needed, what he could use, then send up a smoke message. The Sioux or Crow would use the rest. Gunn leaned his Winchester against the horn with the half twist, then walked back down the wash to get Esquire.

His speed could have taken out both warriors but he knew there were more. Sioux he had neither seen nor heard were standing there waiting for him. He didn't figure they intended to kill him, for if they did, he'd already be dead. One of the warriors was a big man, fully as big as Gunn himself. The other, Gunn judged to be a youth of about fifteen.

"You kill Tatanka Wakan," the big warrior said. "Why?"

Gunn was relieved to hear that the Indian could speak some English. He could get by the with Sioux language in certain tribes, Lakota and Minneconjou for example. But it helped that the other fellow could speak his own lingo.

"Why? To eat," Gunn said. "I lost my pack horse a few days ago."

"One man cannot eat so much," the big warrior said. "You will leave much to go bad."

"No," Gunn insisted. "I was going to make a smoke message to invite others to share the rest."

The warrior looked toward the dead white buffalo, then back at Gunn. His eyes were flashing with hate and anger, more than mere disgust from the waste of a buffalo. Gunn wondered why he was so angry.

"Now, you would steal from us our strength and power. It is not enough that you drive us from our land, kill our children and our young men, violate our women. You steal our God as well."

That was it! Gunn understood now what the warrior meant when he said he had killed Tatanka Wakan. Buffalo God. When he shot the beast he was thinking only of his empty belly. Now he realized he would have been better off had he shot one of the cows. He tried an explanation but it didn't sound too convincing, even to his own ears.

"I took only the meat of the white buffalo," he said. "His power belongs to the Sioux."

The warrior wasn't buying it. He walked over to Gunn and angrily faced him eye to eye.

"No," he said. "He who frees the spirit of the white buffalo has it with him until the day he chooses to die. You have the spirit of the white buffalo."

"I told you," Gunn said. "I don't want your God's medicine. I'll give it back."

"You cannot give it back. I cannot take it from you," the big warrior said. He cupped his hands around his mouth and gave a whoop. Suddenly both sides of the creek bed were lined with more than two dozen Sioux. They were the ones Gunn had felt, rather than seen. "There is one way to see if you speak with straight tongue," the warrior said. "You will come and sit with Sinte Galeshka. He, too, has the spirit of the white buffalo. He will know if you speak the truth."

"I have a job to do," Gunn said.

"I know your job. You carry the words of the Blue Coats." The warrior opened Gunn's saddlebag and removed the Army dispatch case. "You try to protect it with the medicine of the white buffalo, but Sinte Galeshka will read the words and hear your tongue. He will decide if today is the day you choose to die."

Buffalo medicine or not, Gunn knew that he was in no position to argue now. One of the other Sioux held his Winchester while the rest held their weapons pointed toward him. He decided to volunteer the remainder of his good faith. He had his Colt out and reversed before anyone could react.

"All right," he said. "I'll sit with your medicine man or chief or whatever he is." Gunn held his Colt out toward the warrior. "But I'll sit with him as his equal, not as his prisoner." Their eyes locked in a silent battle of will. After several seconds, the warrior took the Colt and, almost imperceptibly, nodded. Gunn knew that he was a prisoner but he'd managed to cast some doubt about it among the Sioux.

The Sioux would understand such things.

A man was only as brave or as big as he thought he was.

The brave man would not fear death.

The wise man did not fear the unknown.

The fearful man could expect that which he feared most to kill him.

From that moment on, Gunn began to think like a Sioux.

## Chapter Two

The village of the Hunkpatila stretched for half a mile along a bend in the Rosebud. This was another of the big gatherings which seemed more and more commonplace now. Gunn knew it meant still more tribes had banded together. Gunn knew if they'd done this forty years ago, America's western boundary would be somewhere near Chicago.

Gunn rode next to the big warrior and that drew everyone's attention. The Sioux women, children and warriors formed lines on both sides of the path.

As he entered the village, Gunn looked at the way it was set up. The outer ring of tipis, six in each circle, housed only unmarried braves. The camp was established for easy defense.

"Sinte Galeshka," the big warrior said. Gunn's eyes shifted along the line of the warrior's pointed finger. He saw a tall, stately looking man. His raven hair was parted in the center and hung straight, flowing down over his broad, muscular shoulders. He wore no head-dress but a bright yellow scarf was tied around his neck. He wore no shirt and instead of a loincloth, was wearing buckskin trousers.

The big warrior dismounted and the two Indians spoke in hushed tones. Gunn was surprised when Sinte Galeshka came toward him. A warrior behind Gunn pushed him. It was a signal for him to dismount. No Sioux chieftain looked up to another man.

Gunn slipped from his saddle and stood there, waiting to see what happened next. Sinte Galeshka sized him up, then studied his face, carefully. Gunn didn't flinch under the gaze.

"I know you, white eyes. You are Shadow Hand. I saw you three winters ago at the Blue Coat fort by the Platte. Your gun brought death to the whites who tried to harm the woman of my son."

Gunn recalled the incident. Three gunnies had set up a trading post outside the fort. They tried to trade the young warrior out of his wife. When that failed, they got nasty. Gunn asked them, nicely, if they would quit. One of them pulled his pistol on Gunn and Gunn wound up shooting them dead. He had already won the name of Shadow Hand among the Sioux, and that day he lived up to it.

"Yes, I remember, Sinte Galeshka," Gunn said. What he didn't say was that he hoped to hell the Indian chief would remember and feel obligated by it.

"You save the woman of my son, but you steal our medicine." Gunn started to speak but the chief's hand darted into the air. "We will not speak of it now." He pointed to the sky, just above the eastern horizon. "When the moon is there, Shadow Hand, we will talk."

The chief spoke in Lakota, speaking so rapidly that Gunn couldn't follow him. Then, before he knew what was happening, his ankles and wrists were bound with rawhide and he was carried away and thrown into a tipi.

"Well, so much for feeling obliged to me," Gunn mumbled. He bellied over to a buffalo robe, then rolled over onto his back. He might as well be comfortable.

The first awareness he had when coming out of sleep was of something warm and soft touching his cheek. It was familiar, but sleep still clouded his brain. The warm softness pressed still harder against his face and something harder, more firm, traced the outline of his mouth. He wet his lips and his tongue brushed against it. There was a muffled giggle. Gunn opened his eyes.

The girl was young, eighteen at most. She was on her knees, straddling Gunn's waist. A few of the setting sun's rays found their way into the dark shadows of the tipi and he could see that she was nude. He caught a glimpse of a tawny-hued shoulder, and a firm bronze breast.

"Off, girl," he said.

The girl reached out to touch his lips, then slipped down to start unbuttoning his shirt.

"Off, I said," Gunn grunted. He bent his legs slightly to gain leverage, then arched his back and tried to buck her off. Her hands found his bare flesh and slid over it. Her fingers explored his nipple, traced a circle around his navel, then dipped lower. She unbuckled his belt and pulled his trousers down as far as she could. He continued to resist, but his protestation lacked its former conviction.

"Untie me," he said.

The girl giggled. Her head dropped to his stomach and she traced a path across it with her tongue. She shifted position, kneeling to one side of him. Her left hand found his cock and squeezed.

"Damn," Gunn said. It was barely more than a whisper, a word surrounded by air exhaled from deep within. She stroked, firmly but gently. She leaned down until her nipple touched his mouth. He nibbled at it and then closed his lips around it and suckled it tenderly.

Gunn could fell himself grow hard. His breathing came in short, rapid spurts of air now and he heard himself moan. Suddenly the breast was gone, the hand stopped. The maiden moved to straddle him again.

Gunn tried to thrust against her but his timing was off. She apparently didn't want him to do anything, but seemed to want to handle it all by herself. She moved up and down on him, slowly at first, then faster, faster and faster. Her hands gripped, kneaded and stroked her own breasts. Feeling her heat, Gunn lost all control, and for a moment he forgot about the leather biting into his wrists.

He arched his back again, his buttocks tightened and the girl let out a little cry, then a moan, then a final sigh. She fell forward against him and they lay for a long time with only the sound of their own breathing between them and the silence.

Gunn didn't know how much time had passed. He was awake suddenly. The weight was no longer there. His eyes adjusted and he saw the Indian girl slipping her buckskin dress over her head. She came back to him, knelt again and reached out with a hunting knife. She smiled and cut through the strips which held his ankles. He rolled to his right and she freed his hands. By the time he was sitting up, she was at the door flap. She looked back. Though the sun had set now there was enough twilight to backlight the girl and he could see her big, brown eyes, her smooth skin, her pouting lips. She smiled at him.

"I am Deer Spirit," she said. "Now I have the man-seed which holds the power of Tatanka."

In his pleasure Gunn had concluded that the girl had been sent to him. Now he wasn't so sure.

Gunn sat quietly for the better part of an hour. The twilight was completely gone now and there was only darkness outside his tent. Finally, the flap opened and a boy stuck his hand in and spoke to him.

"You come now."

When Gunn stepped outside he recognized the boy as being the younger of the two warriors who had discovered him at the buffalo kill. Gunn walked along behind the boy toward the center of the council circle.

The moon was full and hung like a giant lantern above the eastern horizon. There was a fire in the middle of the council circle, so it wasn't all that dark. Gunn could see that most, if not all, of the villagers had been drawn to the center of the village to see what was going to happen.

"You will sit with me, Shadow Hand. We will talk now," Sinte Galeshka said. "By what name are you called by the whites?"

"I am called Gunn." He saw the chief's reaction. My

name is Gunnison," he said. "My Christian name—Gunn is what they call me for short. It has nothing to do with the name the red men know me by."

"Christian," Sinte Galeshka said. "A white man came to me once to teach me to be a Christian. He said nothing about a Christian name."

"It's a different thing," Gunn said. "He wanted to teach you about God."

Sinte Galeshka laughed. "I think it is funny that the white man would teach the Indian about the white man's God. We do not wish to know about these things. White men fight over their God. Indians fight about other things, about land or water or buffalo. But Indians do not fight about the Great Spirit."

"If that is true," Gunn said, "why do you hold me? I killed the white buffalo for meat, not because I wanted his power. He gives me no power."

"If this was true, Shadow Hand, would you tell me of it? Would you sit here in this council with no protection, if you did not have the protection of the white buffalo?"

"I have no protection now. You took my weapons, you tied me up, you can kill me anytime you want to."

"No. If you die, Shadow Hand, it will not be by the word of Sinte Galeshka. You will die if you do not survive the test of the sacred buffalo."

Though there were several Indians gathered nearby, no one sat in the inner council except Gunn and the chief. The chief motioned to the others to join them, but only one came forward.

"Why do only you come to the council, Crippled Antelope?"

"The others will not sit in council with this man. He killed Tatanka. He defiled Deer Spirit. I saw her come from his lodge."

"I sent Deer Spirit to him," the chief said. "Did you not know that?"

"Why did you do such a thing? Now she is like the carcass of a dead buffalo, good only for the scavenger."

"Do not question my reasons," Sinte Galeshka said. "Now, Deer Spirit carries in her the medicine of the white buffalo."

Crippled Antelope remained defiant. He pointed to Gunn. "You had no right to send her to the robes of a white man."

"I, Sinte Galeshka, am chief of the Hunkpatila. I have the right."

"You are the chief. I am the leader of the young men and I speak for the young men when I say that you had no right to defile Deer Spirit."

"You cannot lead where no one will follow," Sinte Galeshka said angrily. He turned to the Indians who were back in the shadows, out of the golden bubble of light from the council fire. "Who among you would follow Crippled Antelope?"

There was no movement.

"Come, who would do so? Those who will, come now, and take your chief and leave the camp of the Hunkpatila."

Gunn got to his feet. If there were going to be trouble he'd already decided his best bet would be to stick with Sinte Galeshka. No one moved.

"You have had your time," the chief said to Crippled Antelope. "Your words are like those spoken in a cave.

They are heard many times but they mean nothing."

"I will have another time," Crippled Antelope said. He moved close to Gunn. "And I will have a time with you, white eyes."

"Could be," Gunn said quietly.

Crippled Antelope stalked away into the shadows and, with his departure, the others gathered in the light of the council fire. The chief sat again across from Gunn.

"Tomorrow, we will test you. If you are false, you will die."

"And if I live?"

"If you live, then the power is with you and you will lie with all the young women of the tribe until each has taken the sacred seed. Then all the children born will grow up to be mighty warriors."

"You mean you have no warriors who have killed a white buffalo?"

"Only I have done this," Sinte Galeshka said. He smiled. "And I have grown too old to visit the robes of the young maidens. I am willing here—" he pointed to his forehead—"and here—" he pointed to his heart. "But I am not able, here." He pointed to his groin.

"I see," Gunn said. "The spirit is willing, but the flesh is weak."

"Yes, yes," Sinte Galeshka said. "That is good, that is very good. The spirit is willing, but the flesh is weak. How do you know to speak such words?"

"They are from the book the Christians use, the Bible," Gunn said. He smiled. "I know a few preachers who'd be a might pissed though, if they knew how I was using the words."

Sinte Galeshka handed Gunn a small cup. "The hot blood of Tatanka will be poured into the cup tomorrow. It is your first test. If the blood doesn't stay within you and mix with the buffalo's spirit, you have failed."

## Chapter Three

Hot buffalo blood wasn't exactly Gunn's idea of an appetizing breakfast. He gagged on the last swallow, but it stayed down. He handed the cup back to Sinte Galeshka.

"What's next?" he asked.

"You will ride a horse that no warrior has been able to ride. If you cannot do this thing, you fail the test."

Gunn hadn't broken a horse since the last one he worked for the Army. Even then it had been broken to the bridle, and it was saddled. This would be barebacked, with nothing but a rope halter to hang on to. Gunn sat down and removed his boots and socks, then he stood up and started moving his arms around, up and down, back and forth, loosening the tightened muscles he would have to call upon for the test.

The stallion was big, a dull white, not quite gray in color. A single rope held its head to a tree. The horse pawed, kicked and snorted. Gunn walked over to him and looked him in the eye.

"All right, you big son of a bitch," he mumbled. "One of us has to break and it damn sure isn't gonna be me."

There was only one way to mount the horse and that

was to vault up on his back. Gunn took a deep breath and jumped. He forked his legs, then when he was mounted, squeezed them tight against the animal's sides. He could feel the stallion's muscles rippling against his thighs, though as yet the horse had made no move. Gunn grabbed a handfull of mane and nodded toward a young buck who was standing nearby. The buck sliced the rope. There were a few seconds of absolute quiet, then all hell broke loose.

Five times the stallion nearly went down. Three times Gunn's grip slipped and he had to put a headlock on the horse's neck.

In one respect it was simple enough—the Sioux had no rules. All he had to do was stay on any way he could. But that was easier said than done.

After trying every vicious maneuver the horse could think of, the animal did a half twist and stopped. He whinnied and pawed and eyed the nearest tree.

"Oh no, you don't, you big son of a bitch," Gunn said.

The stallion seemed to have sprouted wings. Gunn could no longer hear the rhythm of hoof beats, only a solid roar of sound, like distant thunder rumbling through a mountain canyon.

Gunn timed it perfectly and, at the last possible moment swung his left leg into the air, tightening his grip on the stallion's mane like the steel claw of a bear trap. The trunk of the tree became a blur. Gunn's bare feet hit the ground, came up, hit it again, came up a second time and he shifted his weight. He was back on the horse and the stallion kept running, seemingly unable to understand why he couldn't brush this creature off his back as he had done with so many others before.

With the horse now broken to a steady gallop. Gunn gave some consideration to not even trying to turn the steed around. He would ride as far and as fast as the horse would take him. That thought was discarded, though, as soon as he looked around him. He was surprised to see half a dozen warriors on each flank. Now he knew why the cavalry never fared well against the Sioux in a running gunfight. He turned the horse hard, snubbing its nose down with a reaching hand, a hard grip. The Sioux turned with him like spokes on a wheel.

Back in the camp, Gunn made a point of stopping in front of Crippled Antelope. He slid from the big horse.

"He's got no wind left in him," Gunn said. "But he'll get it back. It's just that somebody has to control him."

"Now, Shadow Hand, you will shoot out the eyes of Tatanka and their manitou will give your spirit the power to see."

The Sioux had mounted the white buffalo's head on a tree. Sinte Galeshka led Gunn to a small circle, formed with blood from the buffalo.

"You have only two bullets and you will shoot from here."

It was a fifty-yard shot. Sinte Galeshka had given Gunn his Colt. He was two-thirds of the way to getting to Fort Randall, but this one was about to do him in and he knew it.

"Why do you try to trick me now, Sinte Galeshka?"

The chief was walking away when he heard the words and he turned sharply. "Sinte Galeshka tests you only as he would test a Sioux warrior."

"With a handgun, a gun that has never killed a

24

buffalo? My rifle is the weapon I used, yet you keep it from me now. Do you fear that I will pass your test?"

The chief said nothing, but motioned to a nearby brave. Gunn was given his Winchester and two rounds. He positioned himself, then drew a bead on his target.

"Damn," he growled. "It's still a hell of a shot." He took a deep breath and slowly exhaled it. As he neared the point when he had no air left in his lungs, his index finger began slowly squeezing the trigger. The Winchester barked. A brave ran to the target. A moment later he held up one arm. Gunn glanced at Sinte Galeshka, but the chief showed no expression. There was still an eye to go.

The Winchester barked a second time. Gunn didn't feel this one as he had the first one. He knew the first one was right on, but this one just may have been a bit too high. He watched the brave. The Indian seemed to take forever to examine the head, then he turned around. For a moment he was still, then the left arm went up. A second later, the right arm went up as well. Gunn had hit both of them—he had passed the test.

Gunn spent the rest of the day in the tipi where he enjoyed another visit from Deer Spirit. He wasn't trussed up this time, but just outside, two Hunkpatila braves stood guard.

As much as the chief's words about sharing his power with Sioux maidens appealed to him, Gunn would rather have picked his own time, place and company. Besides, he still had a dispatch for Major Waddington.

The flap to his tipi opened and sunlight poured into the enclosure. Gunn moved his arm from across his eyes and looked up. He was thinking it was about

25

maiden time. Instead, he found he was looking into the face of a warrior. It was a familiar face, and he realized this was one of the men who had brought him in.

"I am Crow King," the warrior said. "I have come to warn you, Shadow Hand. You have passed the test of the sacred buffalo but that will not save your life. There are three more maidens, but if you lie in the robes with Bright Moon, Crippled Antelope will fight you."

"All right, Crow King," Gunn said. "That's fine by me. You just tell Bright Moon not to come in here. I'd just as soon not lie in the robes with anyone else."

"But you must," Crow King said. "If you refuse, Sinte Galeshka will have you killed."

"Well, now, that's a hell of a note," Gunn said. "Seems to me like I'm damned if I do and damned if I don't. Seems to me like you stuck your neck out comin' in here, Crow King, so I'll stick mine out. How do I get the hell out of here?"

"That you cannot do," Crow King said, "unless you are protected by the war shield. Since you carry within you the protection of the sacred buffalo, you would have to fight alongside Lakota warriors. Only then could you ride freely in the land of all Lakota."

"That doesn't sound all that good," Gunn said. "More'n likely I'll be fighting against the Lakota, rather than alongside." Gunn fumbled in his shirt pocket for the makings. He rolled a smoke but didn't light it. Crow King watched in silence, and Gunn looked up at him. "I appreciate what you've told me, Crow King. But why did you?"

"This night in the tipi of my brother, Little Crow, the Shaman will read the bones of the white buffalo you have killed. The bones will tell of things yet to be. Sit with us, so that the Shaman may borrow from your power."

"And Sinte Galeshka? Does he approve of a white man sitting in on a medicine man's doings?"

"He will not know," Crow King said. "Sinte Galeshka rode today to meet with Red Cloud. The Great Father talks of another treaty of peace."

"Yeah. The Great Father does do a heap of talking," Gunn said. He sat up. "All right, Crow King, I'll sit with your Shaman."

Crow King raised his hand. It was a gesture of appreciation. He reached the door and then turned back. "I will come for you when it is time. This night, with Sinte Galeshka away, no maiden will come in the night." Crow King smiled. It was a smile of understanding.

The Hunkpatila medicine man had seen many snows. His face was deeply furrowed and appeared to have the texture of old leather. His eyes, though deep-set in his head, sparkled and missed nothing as he read the bones. He had been chanting and reading for more than an hour. Suddenly, he cast aside all of the bones but one.

*"Tse, wakamani yotanka manitou. Hi ya, hi ya, hi ya."* He scattered some white dust about, then motioned to Gunn. Crow King nudged him and pointed. "Sit there, Shadow Hand."

Gunn took his place and the old Shaman touched the bone to Gunn's forehead. He held it there for more than a minute, then placed the same end on the ground. Gunn watched as the Shaman's arm moved erratically. Lines were drawn and circles and odd shapes and more lines. Crow King leaned forward.

"The bone draws what it saw in the buffalo's spirit," he said to Gunn.

The old Shaman's hand stopped moving. The bone fell from it. He looked up, straight into Gunn's eyes. Gunn was surprised when the old man, who had so far muttered only Sioux phrases, suddenly began speaking in nearly perfect English.

"In five days you will be protected by the Lakota war shield. Within a month, you will ride with your Lakota brothers against the Blue Coats." The Shaman frowned now and lightly touched Gunn's forehead with his finger tips. "A long time, many years from now, you will touch me. Your hair will be as white as the snow on the ground during the winter at Wounded Knee."

The Shaman was finished, and he began chanting in unintelligible phrases again.

"I will tell you what the Shaman said," Crow King offered.

"No need. I understood."

"You can speak our language?" Crow King asked in surprise.

"Hell, he spoke in English."

"No," Crow Kings said. "I heard his words. They were in our language. The Shaman doesn't know English."

"But I heard him. He spoke in English," Gunn said. "Shaman, tell him you spoke in English."

The Shaman spoke, but Gunn didn't understand a word. Crow King listened, then nodded and smiled. He looked at Gunn.

"He says he cannot speak your tongue. The buffalo

spirit in you heard his words, then spoke them in your mind so you could understand."

Gunn left the tipi and went outside. He was puzzled. He knew that the explanation Crow King had just offered was enough to satisfy the Indians, but they were a superstitious lot and could accept such things easily. He could not.

Gunn began thinking about what the Shaman said. The business about snows on the ground at Wounded Knee made no sense but he understood the rest. In less than five days he would fight with the Sioux against their enemies. In less than a month he would ride with them against the Army.

Depending on what he did on those expeditions, one or the other, either the Sioux or his own people, would come to hate him.

It was a hell of a fix to be in, for damned sure.

## Chapter Four

Gunn rolled onto his back and squinted in the semidarkness to identify the visitor. When the visitor spoke, Gunn's ears did what his eyes could not do. It was Crow King.

"You will ride to the hunt, Shadow Hand. The white buffalo's medicine will make the hunt good."

Gunn sat up. It was not yet daylight, but he could see a streak of salmon fringe on the eastern horizon.

"Mind if I wake up first?"

"Come, we ride soon."

Gunn, accompanied by the two big warriors, walked down to the river. He rolled up his shirt sleeves and sloshed the cool water on his face, head and the back of his neck. He heard a giggle and glanced up. Nearby was the most beautiful Indian girl he had ever seen. Her hair glistened, even in the half light. Her eyes were big and dark, but still sparkling. Her features were softly rounded, youthful. She was comely, and then some.

"The maiden is Bright Moon," one of the warriors said when he saw Gunn looking. "She is the chosen one of Crippled Antelope."

"It just might be worth it," Gunn said. He stood up.

"What is it you say, Shadow Hand?"

"Nothing," Gunn replied. He nodded in the direction of Bright Moon and she giggled, looking away shyly.

The sun was still low over the horizon when the Sioux hunting party topped a hill. Below them the Rosebud took a sharp bend and its banks were tree-lined.

"There," Crow King said, pointing to the trees. "It is there we will find the white tails." Crow King held up his hand and Gunn was surprised to see a warrior hand him his Winchester. "You make the first kill. It will bring good medicine to all of us."

The hunting party, about a dozen of them, counting Gunn, fanned out and started down the gently sloping hill, walking their horses. About halfway down a covey of quail suddenly shot up from the reeds along the near bank.

"The Crow!" Crow King shouted. He was right. Twenty, perhaps more, leaped up from concealment alongside the river bank and began firing. Gunn saw two Sioux hit almost at once. There would have been more but only six or eight of the Crow had rifles and those were single-shot Springfields.

The Sioux warriors on the line's flank fell back. Slowly, the line closed into a semicircle, not quite a horseshoe shape. Crow King knew his enemy, the Crow, had spread on either side and were now firing from three directions.

Gunn dropped three of the Crow with as many shots but by now the warriors from both tribes had closed on one another and the fighting became hand to hand. Gunn saw Crow King bring down a warrior with his war club. Then Gunn spotted a Crow with a rifle, lined up straight as a string on Crow King's chest. Gunn snapped off a shot and caught the warrior right between the eyes.

Little Elk, the nephew of Sinte Galeshka, fell to the ground, his head gushing blood. Still he managed to get up and strike out at his attacker, though a second Crow leaped toward the wounded Sioux. Gunn brought the butt of his Winchester up in a wicked arc and dropped one of the Crow. Little Elk buried his knife deep in the chest of the other.

Suddenly Gunn was hit from behind and he rolled along the ground. A Crow warrior jumped on him to count coup, but Gunn managed to duck down and throw the warrior over him. Gunn got back to his feet just as the Crow stood and turned to face him, legs wide apart for balance. It was simply too tempting a target.

The toe of Gunn's boot found its mark, mashing the Indian's testicles and finally striking the pelvic bone. It wasn't a war whoop the Indian sounded, but a shrill shriek of pain. The brave dropped to his knees, then bent over. Gunn retrieved his Winchester and lay the stock across the Crow's right cheek. He heard the bone crack.

Gunn found two more targets to club, then the Crow war party figured they had had enough. They lost three more of their number when Crow King and two other Sioux pursued them to the river's edge. Minutes later, Crow King returned.

"We have lost five," he said. "Little Elk lives." Crow King touched Gunn's forehead. "Only two suns will cross the sky, Shadow Hand, before you are protected by the war shield. When Sinte Galeshka returns, I will tell him of your bravery and your coups."

Two other Sioux were badly wounded and one died before the party returned to the main camp. They had lost half their number, but behind them lay fifteen Crow warriors, and Gunn had taken out eight of them.

As word of the fight spread through the encampment, Gunn heard the young men whooping with delight . . . and the women crying for the dead. Soon, though, the women began gathering wood and preparing the last of the buffalo for a victory celebration.

"Your medicine is strong, Shadow Hand. Truly the white buffalo's manitou protects you. Tonight you will sit at the council fire and the young ones will hear of your fight. Tomorrow you will bite the head of the snake, the heart of the wolf, and the wing of the hawk. Then you will sit with Sinte Galeshka and become his blood brother. You will have the war shield."

Gunn thought of the hot buffalo blood he had been forced to drink and he wondered if he had some other damn fool things to go through. To his relief he learned that the snake, wolf and hawk, were symbolic only.

Throughout the rest of the day he wandered freely among the Sioux, but he couldn't help but notice the two big warriors that were always close at hand. He wasn't a blood brother yet and he decided to play down the fact that much of his strong medicine had come from his Winchester.

## Chapter Five

"Lieutenant Boyer reporting for duty, sir. Two companies, troops C and F, Fifth Cavalry replacements."

Maj. Josiah Waddington finally looked up. "My God," he said. "How old are you, son?"

"I'm twenty-three, sir. Uh, I'll be twenty-three, sir, my next birthday."

"Uh huh. And when, exactly, is that?"

"Just, uh, nine months, sir."

"West Point?"

"Yes, sir!"

"When were you last there?"

"Four months, twenty-one days ago, sir."

Waddington leaned back in his chair and shook his head. "And I'll wager you're the oldest man to ride into Fort Randall today, Lieutenant. Is that right?"

"No, sir. That is, sir, among the enlisted men there is Sergeant Mayhew, sir."

Waddington frowned. "That'd be Benjamin Mayhew?"

"Yes, sir."

Now the major smiled. "Good! He's worth every

other pink-cheeked mother's son you brought with you. Where'd you pick him up?"

"Omaha, sir."

"All right, Lieutenant. You tell my adjutant to find quarters for your, uh, troopers. The missus and I would be honored to have you dine with us this evening. Seven o'clock, Lieutenant."

"Yes, sir. Thank you, sir."

The lieutenant was halfway out the door when the major called to him. "Lieutenant, it isn't the usual procedure but if you have no objections, I'd like Sergeant Mayhew to join us this evening." Waddington had been looking out the window. Now he turned to gauge the young officer's reaction.

"Sir, I . . ."

"Yes, Lieutenant?"

"We were taught that officers shouldn't socialize with—".

"And were you taught to disagree with your commanding officer?"

"No, sir!"

"Then I take it you have no objections if Sergeant Mayhew joins us?"

"No objections, sir."

"Good, Lieutenant. We'll see you this evening."

"Yes, sir," Lieutenant Boyer said, snapping a sharp salute. Waddington returned it with the casualness of his many years of service.

Josiah Benchcroft Waddington was an enigma. He was one of only a handful of regular Army officers who had not served in the Civil War. At fifty-six he had already spent forty years in the Army, more than thirty of them west of the Mississippi. No officer knew the Indian better and damned few were as outspoken. It was, for a career man, his fatal flaw. He had been passed over for promotion more times than he could remember. And the Army didn't hand out field brevets for fighting Indians.

Among Waddington's favorite stories was the time he went east in '63 and was asked by General Grant how he would deal with the Rebs. He looked Grant square in the eye and said, "Let me come back in three months with half a thousand Comanche and I'll show you."

Now, as he looked at the new young men just arrived, he felt sick. He had asked for seasoned troops: they had sent him boys. Not one of these youngsters could stand up to an Indian attack.

"Major?" Waddington turned. The voice belonged to his adjutant, Capt. Fraser Peabody. "Patrol just in, sir. No sign of that dispatch rider."

"Damn! I wonder who they sent out of Robinson?"

"Prob'ly ol' Seth Kinkaid."

The major shook his head. "No, Seth's down at Fort Kearny. Called him down for a meeting with Red Cloud." Waddington rubbed his chin and tugged at his left ear lobe. Those who knew him well never spoke during such times. After a moment, Waddington turned back to Peabody.

"You get a rider out to Robinson with the sun. I don't like big numbers building up between outposts, and I've got a hunch that's just what's happening."

"Could be, Major. Our last patrol reported a lot of smoke signals down along the Rosebud and one of the Crow scouts said it was strong medicine."

"Which Crow?"

"Cut Face."

"Get 'im in here."

A few minutes later Captain Peabody returned with a tall, sullen-looking Crow Indian. He wore buckskin breeches, moccasins and an Army tunic bearing the rank of corporal. Waddington and the Indian spoke in the Indian's language, while Captain Peabody looked on. Finally Waddington waved the scout away. "I was afraid of that," he said.

"Sorry, sir, but I could only catch part of it."

"Red Cloud is an old woman, so says our Crow friend. Worse, more and more of the Sioux are thinking that way. The Department of the Missouri is still trying to wrest more land away from them up in the Black Hills. It's their sacred ground, the Paha Sapa, they call it. Now, there's another tribe involved, the Hunkpatila. They used to stay up north, nearer the Canadian border. Now, according to Cut Face, there's a sizable number of 'em down here under a tough old bird named Sinte Galeshka."

"Why? Why come south from a territory that's pretty much free of the white men?"

"Because they've been invited."

"Invited?"

"Yep. That's been the big danger, you know, ever since Fremont first come out here, that all Indians, no matter their heritage, no matter their differences, would band together."

"And fight together?" Peabody asked.

"Yep."

"My God, sir. Why, it would take—"

"Don't even try to calculate it, Fraser, because we don't have enough men. Not here, not now, and not for a very long time."

"Then we can't let the Indians get together."

"You got that right," Waddington said.

Both Major Waddington and his wife Ellie were hard pressed to keep from laughing at the young lieutenant's discomfort. It resulted from the less-than-gracious table manners displayed by Sergeant Mayhew. They, of course, were used to it. Mayhew had served some ten years, off and on, with the major. Mercifully, the meal finally ended.

"Coffee, Lieutenant?"

"Yes'm. Thank you."

"Cigar, son?"

"Uh, no, sir, thank you, sir," Boyer said.

"Relax, Lieutenant," Waddington said. "I like to get to know the officers that serve with me."

"Yes, sir."

"You ever fight an Indian?"

"No, sir."

Sergeant Mayhew carefully centered a wad of chewing cud in his mouth, puckered his lips and spat juice, dead center, into the big, brass spittoon. It made a ringing sound.

"You ever seen an Injun, sir?" Mayhew asked.

"Oh, yes, Sergeant. There were several of them in Washington about two years ago. They were brought to the Point for a special appearance."

"Is that right? Must've been downright dangerous,"

Mayhew said. He spit again, this time more in contempt than need.

"You told me you were twenty-three," Waddington said, "or almost that. Can you ride bareback, full speed, hanging on only with the strength of your legs and fire a rifle, accurately, at the same time?"

"Of course not, sir."

"An Indian boy no more than half your age can do that. He can fire an arrow straight into the heart of a buffalo, both animals running full speed."

"Can you swing your body so low and close to one side of a pony runnin' top speed that you can't be seen?" Mayhew asked.

"No, Sergeant, I can't."

"Injun can."

"Can an Indian compute the trajectory and bursting radius of a piece of field artillery?" Boyer asked with wounded pride.

"Don't need to," Mayhew answered. "They don't use them things. They do use ponies and rifles."

"Tell me, Sergeant, can you do all those things?"

"No, sir," the sergeant said easily.

"Then what is your point?"

"The point is that them what can do all them things, makes better fighters than them that can't."

"Surely, Major Waddington, you don't believe that the Indian is a superior soldier to the man in the ranks of the United States Army?" Boyer was looking for support that he felt sure he wasn't going to find.

"Let me put it this way, Lieutenant. If I could have just one Comanche, or Sioux, or Cheyenne, for every five cavalrymen I've got here, I might just whip this frontier into shape."

"With all due respect, Major, I have to disagree. I recently attended a staff briefing at which one of the Army's finest field officers spoke. He concluded by stating that given a regiment of United States Cavalry he could ride rampant over the entire Sioux nation."

"You recollect his name, do you, Lieutenant?"

"I do, Sergeant Mayhew. It was Custer. George Armstrong Custer."

"Well, sir, remember it, 'cause if'n he ever was to try such a damn fool stunt, I'll wager you'd not be hearin' from him again."

The major's wife, perhaps for the best, interrupted the conversation, "Your adjutant is here, Josiah."

"Send him in, Ellie."

Captain Peabody looked stern. He eyed both the lieutenant and Sergeant Mayhew but said nothing.

"Go ahead, Fraser. Whatever it is, they'll know soon enough."

"A massacre, sir. Six wagons, about thirteen people." The major got to his feet. Ellie Waddington clamped her hand to her mouth. "Three wagons got away. Someone came to their rescue but they don't know who it was. They made it back here."

"Where'd it happen, Fraser? When?"

"Early this morning, down along the Rosebud."

"Know what Injuns done it, Cap'n?" Mayhew asked.

"No, Sergeant. These people broke off from a big train that's well to the south of here. They've no one with them to guide or warn them. Certainly no one with any Indian experience."

"We'll get a patrol out at first light, Fraser." The

major walked over and put his hand on his wife's shoulder. "And a burial detail."

"Yes, sir."

"Gentlemen, I'm sorry, but the evening is at an end."

It was just past ten o'clock the next morning when Captain Peabody came into Major Waddington's office. "A dispatch rider just came in from the south, sir," he said, handing Waddington the message.

Order out a company for escort duty. Thirty-five-wagon caravan must be routed north along the Rosebud. Cannot afford to disrupt council with Chief Red Cloud.

J. L. Tapeley
General Command
Department of the Missouri

"They've gone completely mad, risking the lives of unarmed settlers up here so they can lie to Red Cloud down there."

"Sir?"

"Did you get that patrol out?"

"Yes, sir, and the rider to Fort Robinson."

"Good. All right, Fraser, send me that new lieutenant, Boyer. If the real trouble stays west, maybe he can ride escort to at least get that train up here."

"What are we going to do about the incident on the Rosebud?"

"Once the wagon train is safe, we'll mount three companies and see if we can flush out any offenders."

"Yes, sir."

Waddington tried to conceal his worry.

But his gut tightened into a knot and the frown on his face seemed permanently etched.

The whole frontier was like a powder magazine. Something like this could make it blow up in his face.

## Chapter Six

The council fires could be seen for miles and Gunn had never witnessed an Indian ceremony with more pomp and pageantry. The two central fires, some fifty yards apart, were each ringed by three smaller ones. The parent tribes were represented by the larger blazes. They were the Teton and the Oglala. All the plains Sioux were represented, including the Brule, Sans Arc, Minneconjous, Hunkpapa and Sinte Galeshka's Hunkpatila. Only the woodland tribe of the Santee was missing. The great plains tribes held their woodland cousins in contempt, for the Santee had yielded to the white man's encroachment.

Gunn had been initiated with the snake, the wolf and the hawk. Now all that remained was the final approval of the key leaders and the act of mingling his blood with that of the tribal chieftain in whose tribe Gunn had shown his bravery.

"You will stand now, before the council," Gunn was told. Crow King walked with him to the circle of power. The warrior stood by his side because it was he who would tell of Gunn's bravery.

"Only one other white man is brother to all Sioux.

So you shall be, Shadow Hand, if the sacred circle so speaks. I, Sinte Galeshka, am the first to speak. I say it shall be."

One of the other Indians spoke then. "I am Hawk Who Hunts Walking. I say it shall be so."

"I am American Horse. I say it shall be so."

"I am Kicking Bear. I say it shall be so."

"I am Short Bull. I say it shall be so."

Suddenly a voice came from outside the circle, back in the shadows. "I, Crippled Antelope say no! I say death to the white eyes!"

Sinte Galeshka leaped to his feet. "You dare to violate the sacred circle and mock the ceremony of the blood brother? You have no say in this, Crippled Antelope."

The big warrior nevertheless pushed his way through to the circle's center. He stood there and looked around defiantly, as if challenging anyone to stop him from speaking.

"You are blinded by the death of the Crow. You are weak, like a woman, and crazy like you would be from drinking fire water."

"Silence!" Sinte Galeshka said. "Another of your words will bring you death."

"Then I shall die the death of a warrior, not that of an old woman."

Sinte Galeshka, with surprising quickness for a man of his age, drew his knife and lunged toward Crippled Antelope. Gunn stepped in between.

"No! I can't let a man die for speaking his piece," Gunn said. "Not even to become a blood brother of the Lakota."

"You are not yet a brother," Sinte Galeshka reminded

him.

"And I won't be if you kill him."

"I do not hide behind a white man's words," Crippled Antelope said. Gunn whirled to face him.

"I'm not doing it for you, friend," Gunn said menacingly. "I'm doing it for me. I've had about one push too many from you."

"Then fight me, white man, and let the sacred buffalo decide our fate," Crippled Antelope challenged, grinning broadly.

The huge, bone handle of Crow King's knife settled the matter. He brought it down on Crippled Antelope's head and Crippled Antelope slumped into a heap at Sinte Galeshka's feet.

"I have claimed my right as the warrior brother of Shadow Hand. I, alone, will decide the fate of Crippled Antelope, but not now, not before the sacred ceremony is done."

"When the sun is straight over the violated ground you shall decide then," Sinte Galeshka said.

Crippled Antelope was bound with strips of hide, tied to a lodgepole outside the circle, where he would remain until noon the next day. Now, Gunn and Sinte Galeshka sat facing one another, each with his right arm thrust forward. A moment later Crow King slashed a gash in their arms, just above the wrists. They touched and the blood flowed together.

After fifteen minutes, Deer Spirit and Bright Moon came forward and separated the men's arms. They treated each with herbs and medicines. Then, Sinte Galeshka and Gunn stood and they gripped hands, their right arms upright in front of them.

"Now, Shadow Hand, you are as Crow King, as

Little Elk, as Spotted Tail, and as all these men. You are a Lakota warrior and you are my brother. You may ride among all our people as brother, and are protected by the spirit of the white buffalo and the sacred war shield."

Gunn was uneasy for the rest of the ceremony. Maidens danced and Sioux warriors worked themselves into a frenzy to draw from Gunn's power. He could think of little else but Crippled Antelope's plight. He reckoned that with morning he would try to use his new power, whatever it was, to influence Crow King into making the right decision. Gunn didn't like Crippled Antelope, but he understood him.

It was late before Crow King led Shadow Hand to his own tipi. It bore the special markings of the white buffalo and would always be with the Hunkpatila, used by no one unless Shadow Hand approved.

"I'm curious, Crow King," Gunn said. "Sinte Galeshka said only one other white man was brother to all the Sioux. Who is he?"

"The one you call Bridger."

"Jim Bridger?"

"Yes."

"Yeah," Gunn said. "It figures."


This time Gunn's feet and hands weren't bound and he wasn't asleep. He had rolled a smoke and was deep in thought when the buffalo hide moved and the moonlight played over the form of a woman.

"I have come to you, great warrior. Through my body our spirits will meet and I will receive the power to mother a great Lakota leader."

Bright Moon was even more beautiful tonight than she had been when he first saw her on the bank of the river. He crushed out his cigarette and pushed away the fleeting thought of Crippled Antelope's claim on this woman. Right now, he didn't give a damn.

Bright Moon's body was firm, its bronze tones alternately highlighted by the application of scented oils. Her breasts were not large but they jutted nearly straight out from her chest and were tipped by dark, hardened nipples.

Gunn felt a tingling sensation as they came together. His hands found her breasts and traced a path down along her velvet flesh. She pushed gently against him and they eased themselves onto the thick, soft, buffalo hides. Deer Spirit's ministrations earlier had urged him to a quick climax, a response to something immediate. But Bright Moon was a woman making love to him, and fulfilling some urgent need of her own.

Bright Moon was not hurried as her tongue circled his nipples, his navel, then found the hardened rod of his manhood. She played her lips and tongue over his taut muscles, arousing him beyond reason.

She raised her head and Gunn could see the expression in her eyes. Was she good enough? As good as a white woman? He raised himself, wishing to answer with action rather than words. She moved her body next to his and lay back. His hands found her breasts, his fingers stroked her nipples. Bright Moon's lips parted and she breathed a long sigh. Her body tensed as Gunn's hands stroked and explored.

"No warrior has touched me in this way," she whispered as Gunn's fingers probed her most intimate, sensitive spots.

"Go inside me, now!" Bright Moon said. She wasn't begging, it was more of a demand. "I can wait no longer," she moaned.

Gunn withdrew his fingers. He moved quickly but gently. The quiver of her response began as he entered her and spread through her body. She trembled. She arched her back to meet him.

In the back of Gunn's mind he knew he could die here if Crippled Antelope found them. He didn't care. Fingers clawed his back. Their lips met, burned. Bright Moon moaned and dug her fingers into Gunn's shoulders. Their bodies exploded.

Oily body fluids mixed with sweat now turned cool. No sound but their own breathing could be heard. A minute, then two, passed, and Gunn realized that he was still inside her, still hard, imprisoned by a vise of flesh.

Bright Moon tensed again, and Gunn responded. Their passion erupted a second time before both were spent.

"No woman, white or red, has ever satisfied me more," Gunn told her. She smiled. It was a woman's smile, the smile of any woman who had just given her all and had been found satisfactory. "Did you do all this only to acquire my medicine?"

Bright Moon got to her feet. She stood over him, her nakedness still appealing, even at his passion's lowest ebb.

"This time," she said, "it was for the power. Next time it will be for Bright Moon."

Gunn dragged deeply on his smoke. He thought himself a damned fool. He had a job to do and he wasn't doing it. Hell, he wasn't even trying. It wasn't so much out of loyalty, or even duty to the Army. It was Gunn himself. He had become lax. That could be fatal. He knew being a blood brother to the Sioux could be helpful, but he also knew he had to get on with his own life. He was, after all, a white man, not an Indian, and his name was Gunn, not Shadow Hand.

# Chapter Seven

Little Bear bellied his way to the top of the ridge. Below him the small buffalo herd grazed quietly. He smiled. It was his first opportunity to lead a hunting party of young warriors. The six young men would bring home much meat and he would prove himself. Then he would become a hunter of the Crow instead of buffalo.

Little Bear hurried back to the others. "The herd is here," he said, smiling broadly and pointing back in the direction from which he had come.

The first shot ended Little Bear's life instantly, snuffing him out while his smile still clung to his lips. The others followed him shortly thereafter. The Army had come upon them from both sides and there were just too many.

"Major Waddington oughta be mighty pleased about this," Lt. Fred Jefferson said as he walked around the dead Indians, poking at their still-warm bodies with his saber.

"You reckon these here is the ones that attacked those settlers?" Corporal Flynn asked. Corporal Flynn was new to the West and the brief, bloody fight had been terribly exciting to him. He hadn't said anything to the others, but his blood raced when they opened fire. If this was all there was to Indian fighting, he was going to like it out here. He was going to like it a lot.

"Hell, yes, they're the ones. Couldn't be anyone else," Lieutenant Jefferson said.

Pvt. Josh Tapley dismounted and knelt beside the body of Little Bear. He turned the young Indian over and examined him for a moment, then stood up.

"Beggin' your pardon, Lieutenant," he said. "But these bucks are Sioux, not Crow. And they're hunters, not warriors. They don't even show the markings of a warrior. I'm afraid we've killed the wrong ones. My guess is these are Hunkpatila Sioux."

Jefferson's head jerked around toward Tapley, then he frowned. "Mount up, Tapley," he snarled. "You're not a scout anymore. If I want your advice or opinion, I'll ask for it."

Josh Tapley had probably sent more Indians to the Great Spirit than Lieutenant Jefferson had ever seen, and fought more battles than Jefferson had imagined. Though not a graduate of West Point, as was his brother, Josh had served as a Brevet Major General in the Confederate Army.

Since the war his brother had offered once or twice to help Josh get a commission, but Josh wanted nothing to do with it. In truth, he couldn't even hold on to a non-commissioned officer's stripes now, because he had what many called the "soldiers' disease." He was an incurable alcoholic. He was nearly fifty now, and would probably never have another stripe on his sleeve.

As the column headed east toward the fort, Josh's eyes scanned every foot of ground on either side.

Somewhere out there was one more Sioux, an observer who was, even now, watching every move the Army made. Josh didn't see him, but he felt that he was there.

Josh was right. The lone Sioux was a boy on his very first hunting trip. Little Bear's brother stayed well hidden until the last of the Army column's dust had drifted out of sight. Then, Eagle Claw mounted his new pony, hunkered down against its back and rode, hell bent, for the Hunkpatila camp.

Lt. Calvin Boyer walked to the center of the largest of the three circles of wagons. A tall, burly man wearing buckskins met him.

"You come to take us north, Lieutenant?"

"I did, sir. Lieutenant Calvin Boyer at your service. I urge you to move quickly to organize the train. Are you the wagonmaster?"

"I am. Seth Ledbetter's the name, late of the Missouri Volunteers." He extended a big, meaty palm.

"I've heard your name," Boyer said. "I assume you know what happened up north."

"I do, but I was of the understandin' the Army was meetin' with ol' Red Cloud to try 'n' get somethin' worked out."

"I believe that is correct, sir, but there has been trouble up on the Rosebud. We're not sure just what Indians did it."

"Crow did it, Lieutenant. I rode up there and had me a look-see. Just got back this mornin'."

"We've had trouble with the Sioux as well. Can't be sure."

"Maybe you can't be sure, Lieutenant, but I am. They was Crow, no doubt."

"I understand they were run off. I mean, whoever attacked the wagons."

"They was. Sioux run 'em off. They's no love lost between them two, I can attest to that. Sioux don't want no trouble, though, they just want to be left alone. You Army folks better learn that. They's room fer ever'body out here if you talk straight."

"It would seem the Crow, if it was Crow, don't agree."

"That's just a few, son. We get rid of a few bad apples, white man and red, and we'll be able to ride through this country and camp with the Indians."

"Perhaps you're right, sir, but for now—"

"Don't fret none, boy. We'll be ready in an hour."

Lt. Fred Jefferson eyed Sergeant Mayhew with some contempt as he brushed by him. Jefferson had just finished his report to Major Waddington. The major looked up. "Come in, Sergeant. I'd like to ask you a few questions about the report I just got."

"That's what I come in for, Major. I jist finished talkin' to Josh Tapley. He rode out with the lieutenant."

"Josh Tapley's a hopeless drunk," Jefferson spouted. "Why, even the fact that his brother is commanding the department can't get his stripes back."

"Bein' a drunk don't make him dumb," Mayhew said. "He knows Injuns, especially what kind is what kind."

"What do you mean?" Major Waddington asked.

"Accordin' to Josh, the lieutenant and his men here massacred a huntin' party o' boys this mornin'," Mayhew said. "They wasn't even Crow, they was

Hunkpatila Sioux boys. They's no way they coulda been the ones that shot up them sod busters."

"Is Josh drunk or sober?"

"You know Josh, Major. It's hard to tell anymore."

"You think he knows what he's sayin'?"

"Yes, sir. I'd be willin' to stake my life on it."

Major Waddington sighed, then stood up and reached for his tunic. "What's done is done," he growled. "Come along with me. Oh, and you can bring Tapley along if you wish to."

"Major, what are we up to?"

"We're gonna skin us a bear," Major Waddington said.

"You wouldn't be about to skin the wrong bear, would you?"

"Perhaps I am. But it's my firm belief, Sergeant Mayhew, that all the bears are going to have to be skinned sooner or later."

"I reckon so, sir. But you got to kill 'em first. Once you get that done, the rest's easy.

## Chapter Eight

Gunn came from his tipi when he heard the ruckus. He picked up a few words here and there but he finally had to pull Crow King aside to find out what was going on. He knew only that he was in a village of too damned many Indians.

"What is it?" he asked. "What's going on?"

"Little Bear is dead. Running Turtle and Buffalo Horn, too."

"The boys who went out on the hunting party?"

Crow King nodded.

"What was it, the Crow?"

"Pony soldiers."

"Couldn't be," Gunn said. "The Army's got no reason to kill Hunkpatila."

Crow King rolled his lips back from his teeth. "The Blue Coats need no reason to kill Indians, Shadow Hand. It is reason enough that we are Indians."

"Oh, no, not Major Waddington. He'll carry out his orders in a big fight, but he wouldn't send troopers out against a bunch of boys on a hunting trip."

"Then why did they die, Shadow Hand?"

Gunn whirled. Sinte Galeshka stood behind him. "I

". . . I reckon I can't answer that," he said, surprised at the uncertainty in his own tone.

"You will free Crippled Antelope," Sinte Galeshka said. "He will lead the young men against the Blue Coats. You must wait to claim your right against him, Crow King."

The big warrior's eyes shifted, briefly, to Gunn, but he nodded and walked off.

"You can't just attack the Army, Sinte Galeshka," Gunn said. "You'll start a war nobody wants. Let me ride to the fort and find out what happened."

"It's too late," Sinte Galeshka said. "What must be done will be done."

"You go ahead and do what you have to," Gunn said. "But I have to do the same."

"You will not leave the village of the Hunkpatila until you have done the things the Shaman saw."

"You know?"

"I am the chief, Shadow Hand. I know all things of the village."

"And I'm a blood brother. Does the Hunkpatila refuse his blood brother freedom?"

"You may walk among all Sioux in spirit and in flesh, Shadow Hand, after the Shaman's words are proven true."

"I'm no blood brother. I'm a prisoner, nothing more."

"You are a Lakota warrior who carries in his heart the spirit of the sacred buffalo. Defile the sacred law and the Shaman's vision and you will bring evil upon the Hunkpatila until all those now living are gone. You will not do this thing."

Sinte Galeshka walked away and Gunn knew the only way he would make it to the fort was to escape.

Less than half an hour later Gunn saw the young warriors painting their faces and bodies with the sacred symbols of war. There would be a brief war dance, then they would ride off to do battle.

As Gunn watched the preparations being made, he realized that he was, once again, under guard. This time there were three warriors posted. Gunn went back inside his tipi and rolled a smoke. He knew he'd have to bide his time, but if there was to be peace along the Rosebud, it was not up to Gunn to keep it.

Gunn had dozed off when he was suddenly awakened by the kick of a heavy foot. He jerked awake and saw Crow King.

"You will come to the lodge of Sinte Galeshka," Crow King said. He hurried away and Gunn followed a few minutes later. Inside Sinte Galeshka's tipi, Gunn saw a large Indian he hadn't seen before.

"This is Kicking Bird," Sinte Galeshka said. "He is the leader of the Oglala Hunkpatila. His warriors came upon white men and wagons. They were with women and children and they were being attacked by Crow. Kicking Bird's warriors drove off the Crow but most of the whites were killed. Kicking Bird believes Little Bear's hunters died because the Blue Coat soldiers thought they were the white men's killers. Is this thing possible, Shadow Hand?"

"Yeah," Gunn said. "More than possible, likely."

"Why would the pony soldiers kill before they know the truth?"

"Same reason your warriors are planning to ride out now, Sinte Galeshka," Gunn said. "You telling me they'll make sure they've got the right soldiers before they start shooting?"

"All white men are enemies," Kicking Bear said contemptuously.

"Then kill me," Gunn snapped. "I may be a blood brother, but I am still white."

"We were told there would be no more wagons of white men on the Rosebud. The Great Father sent his word with Bearcoat Miles. Wagons would stay along the Platte in the land of the Oglala of Red Cloud. That was a lie."

"Look," Gunn said to Kicking Bear. "I know you've been lied to, but not even the Army can control every white man, any more than you can control every Indian. Those whites paid for their mistake but that's no reason to bring a war down on yourselves." Gunn looked Kicking Bear straight in the eye. "You can't win. Ride to the fort with me and we'll tell them what happened. Major Waddington will listen. He doesn't want a war with the Hunkpatila."

"I have told you, Shadow Hand," Sinte Galeshka said. "It is too late. Even now the young men under Crippled Antelope ride to the hills."

"You told me the chiefs have spoken, but if Kicking Bear brings back the truth from the fort, will they listen and speak again?"

Sinte Galeshka stood and turned to Kicking Bear. "It is for you to speak of this thing. Do you wish it?"

"I wish only to be left alone on my land. I heard the voice of Bearcoat Miles and I sat in council with Red Cloud and the Oglala and the Teton. If no wagons come to the Rosebud, then there will be no fight with the pony soldiers."

"Then you'll ride with me to the fort?" Gunn asked.

"No. I'll send my son and ten warriors. They will

carry my words and yours, Shadow Hand."

"And I, too, will send ten warriors and my son," Sinte Galeshka said. "If they return with the Blue Coat major's promise, the chiefs will hear it and speak again."

Gunn didn't like the compromise, particularly since he was still carrying a dispatch for Major Waddington. Still, it beat the hell out of an all-out war along the Rosebud.

"Will you allow me to write down my words, explain where I've been, and send on my dispatch, the talking paper?"

"Yes."

Kicking Bear left the lodge then and Gunn started to follow. Sinte Galeshka touched his shoulder and Gunn turned back. "This will only add to the fire of hate which burns in the heart of Crippled Antelope," he said.

"I've run up against white men who are the same way," Gunn replied. "Can't keep everybody happy now, can we?"

"His hate is deep, Shadow Hand, and he has been shunned by Bright Moon. He is a strong warrior and he has never lost a fight."

"Thanks for the warning," Gunn said. "I'll keep that in mind if it comes to it."

## Chapter Nine

White Horse Standing couldn't believe his eyes. Below him, stretched out for as far as he could see, a wagon train wound lazily through the country. Some of the wagons had already crossed the shallow ford on the Rosebud known as Two Elms crossing. Now they formed up, awaiting their companions.

White Horse Standing could also see the Army sentries posted to guard the wagons. Sinte Galeshka had told his son to ride out with Young Bull, the son of Kicking Bear, and to avoid fighting with the pony soldiers. If there was to be a fight, he was to ride back to the village. Young Bull had received the same instructions.

White Horse Standing rode quickly back to the others.

"Pony soldiers and white men's wagons," he said to Young Bull. He placed the tips of his fingers together, then separated his hands and arms as far apart as possible to indicate how long the wagon train appeared to be.

"Where?"

"At the water of Two Elms on the Rosebud."

"Then the white eyes have spoken with two tongues and the one called Shadow Hand has also. We will return to your father's village and all the Hunkpatila will ride against the Blue Coats and their wagons."

The warriors mounted their ponies and followed a dry wash back down the ridge to the river. There, among the cover of the trees, they cooled themselves and watered their animals. That done, they would ride hard for home.

"I made out about twenty of 'em, Major," Sergeant Mayhew said. "They was too far away for me to see any war paint, but I don't figure a huntin' party this far south."

Major Waddington stood in his stirrups and looked to see how the river crossing was progressing. He hadn't planned to take a force against the Indians until the wagon train was safely ensconced at Fort Randall, but he had grown increasingly concerned about Lieutenant Boyer's youth, and the failure of the original dispatch rider to arrive from Fort Robinson.

"Sergeant, take troop E and ride east until you're clear of that stand of timber along the river. Form a skirmish line along the ridge and I'll drive those Indians to you."

"They may just be a decoy, Major."

"Yes, Sergeant, they may be. I'll hit them with troop C and hold troop B in reserve, here on the ridge. If it turns out there are more, return here and we'll pull back together down to the river. The main thing is to keep ourselves between whatever Indians may be out there and that wagon train."

"Yes, sir."

For once, Major Waddington's experience had caught the small band of Hunkpatila completely by surprise. The fifty troopers, split into three groups, struck without warning. Waddington himself led twenty men, on foot, into the trees. They fanned out and opened the attack. Smaller groups, at either end of the Indians' gathering point, charged them on horseback.

Young Bull fell, mortally wounded, and six other warriors died in that first deadly onslaught. White Horse Standing knew there was no chance against the Blue Coats. Elk Man rushed to him.

"The Blue Coats have charged through us, there," he said, pointing west. "We can flee."

White Horse Standing looked. It was true. Now the soldiers came on foot through the trees and the others regrouped to the east. To the west there were no soldiers.

"No! It's a trap! We must cross the river!" White Horse Standing slipped from his mount and slapped the pony's flank. "Run your horses into the trees! Run them into the Blue Coats!" he shouted. He turned to run toward the river, then heard the sickening sound of a bullet striking bone and flesh. Elk Man's body spun nearly around, then he fell face down.

Out of the corner of his eye, White Horse Standing could see other warriors splashing into the river. Here, the current was stronger but they must fight it. They must not be carried downstream to where the wagons were crossing. Yellow Moon's body stiffened and White Horse Standing could see the twisted shape of his face as the bullet struck him, high on his back.

White Horse Standing felt sick with grief and filled with hate at the same time. Only eight of the Hunkpatila reached the opposite shore without wounds. Three others made it, but only one of them would live.

Only two soldiers had been killed. Sergeant Mayhew and his company rejoined the main body.

"Do we give chase, Major?"

"No, Sergeant. Not now, but it's obvious we've got them on the run. Send a man back to the fort and bring two more companies."

"But, sir, that'll leave the fort with only one troop."

"Two, Sergeant. Lieutenant Boyer's troop will return with the wagon train. We'll camp with it tonight, and tomorrow ride west to finish the job."

"Major, can I speak my mind?" Sergeant Mayhew asked.

Major Waddington chuckled. "When in the hell haven't you, Sergeant?"

"Them was Sioux we just shot up. Hunkpatila Sioux. They was too few for fightin' and too many for huntin' this far south."

"Then what were they doing here?"

"Don't rightly know, Major," the old sergeant said. "But they just mighta been comin' in to palaver with you. If that was the case, we won't be gettin' off so easy the next time."

"None of it is easy, Sergeant Mayhew. I don't like this any better than you do." Waddington took a deep sigh and shook his head. "Lying goes against everything I was ever taught, but you and I can't stop progress."

"No, sir, I reckon not. But I can't help wonderin' if them folks in Washington sometimes might get just a little confused."

"About what, Sergeant?"

"About the difference between progress and greed."


Gunn ducked low to enter Sinte Galeshka's tipi. It didn't take him long to realize he was in the middle of a bunch of angry Indians.

"What's wrong?" Gunn asked.

"Only my blood flowing with yours spares your life, Shadow Hand."

"And even that will not spare you now, white eyes." Gunn turned to see Crippled Antelope. "I have claimed my right to gather the warriors who will ride against the Blue Coats tomorrow. I have chosen you to ride with me."

Gunn ignored Crippled Antelope's words and turned back to Sinte Galeshka.

"What happened?"

"The Blue Coats had wagons at the Rosebud . . . many wagons. When our warriors saw them, they attacked. The son of Kicking Bear is dead. So is Elk Man and Yellow Moon."

"Damn," Gunn said. He shook his head. "I don't know what the hell is going on here, Sinte Galeshka, but if you attack Fort Randall it will only make things worse."

"We will speak no more of these things, Shadow Hand. You will ride against the pony soldiers at the side of Crippled Antelope."

"No," Gunn said. "I won't do that."

"Then you will die here, white eyes. I will kill you," Crippled Antelope said.

"And if you are victorious and defeat Crippled Antelope, and still refuse to ride with us, I shall order your death so that the spirit of the white buffalo is freed from an enemy of our people," Sinte Galeshka said.

Gunn stood there, stripped to the waist and barefooted. The Sioux war club was lashed to his right wrist with a strip of hide from the white buffalo. He stepped from his tipi and saw that the council fire was burning brightly, its flames nearly ten feet tall at the center. A soft hand touched his bare back.

"Do not turn," Bright Moon whispered. "Fight Crippled Antelope, but do not kill him. You are a Lakota brother. You, too, have a right to claim. If you defeat him, tell Sinte Galeshka you have struck him with the sacred buffalo's spirit and you wish him to ride for you."

"And if I do kill him?"

"You will die at the hand of Kicking Bear."

"I won't ride against the Army."

"You must if you win the fight. They won't give you weapons. Only the sacred buffalo and the war shield will protect you. It will be your only hope, your only chance to help your Sioux brothers and your white brothers." The hand disappeared and so did Bright Moon. Gunn walked to the council fire.

Six warriors danced around Crippled Antelope. They feigned counting his enemy's coup and they touched his war club with the sacred feathers and the bones of the white buffalo. No one stood with Gunn or danced for his victory, not even Crow King.

The dancing stopped. The Shaman tossed a mixture

of crushed bone and gunpowder into the council fire and the flash signalled the beginning of the fight.

Gunn circled cautiously. Somehow, Crippled Antelope looked even bigger to him. The rippling muscles of his body were highlighted even more by the shadows of the dancing flames. Crippled Antelope's war club swished through the night air, inches from Gunn's head. He bobbed his head and parried with carefully placed counterstrokes.

The big Sioux brought the club high over his head and darted forward. Gunn backed off but suddenly the Indian dropped to his knees and the club lashed out at Gunn's ankles. It grazed a shin and Gunn felt the pain. A full blow would have broken his leg. He sidestepped and circled again. Crippled Antelope moved in.

Gunn shifted the war club in front of himself. It was horizontal, at waist level. Crippled Antelope's eyes dropped to it and Gunn struck, his left fist landing hard on the Sioux's jaw. The Indian's head snapped back and he staggered. Gunn made his move. Head lowered, he butted into the Indian's belly.

Crippled Antelope grunted and lost his footing. Gunn struck again with his left fist, snapping Crippled Antelope's head to the side. Gunn rolled and came to his feet. The Indian was only half up. The club landed on the Indian's right shoulder, just above the shoulder muscle. Gunn's arm withdrew and he struck again, a backhand swing. He pulled it at the last moment. The club's force knocked the big Indian senseless but didn't crush his skull. He dropped in a thunking heap at Gunn's feet.

Gunn dropped to his knees beside the unconscious warrior. He took Crippled Antelope's knife from its sheath and held it above his head.

"I claim my right as a blood brother of Sinte Galeshka." Gunn cut through the rawhide holding his war club to his wrist. He took the club and touched it to Crippled Antelope's chest. "Through this weapon, the weapon of the victor over Crippled Antelope, I place the spirit of the sacred buffalo in Crippled Antelope's heart. He will ride into battle protected and he will not again stand against Shadow Hand."

"You have spoken as a Lakota warrior and you have fought well. I, Sinte Galeshka, say this thing to you. Your right is honored, but you must ride against the Blue Coats, armed only with the weapon of your heart and war shield."

Back in the darkness of his tipi, Gunn felt a knot in his stomach. He rolled a smoke and lay in the quiet of the night, his forearm across his eyes, pondering his fate with the coming of a new day. He was able to sum it all up in a single utterance.

"Shit," he said.

# Chapter Ten

The last notes of mess call were still hanging in the air when Maj. Josiah Waddington snapped the button on his tunic collar and stepped out of his headquarters tent. The regimental trumpeter was putting his horn back in his saddlebags when Waddington looked toward him.

Beyond the bugler, Waddington could see down into the valley of the Rosebud and the wagon train where dozens of children were scurrying around and women were hunched over cookpots. From the wagon train and from the Army encampment, dozens of streamers of white smoke curled into the warm, morning air, clearly marking their position for anyone who might be interested.

"Mornin', Major." It was the voice of Captain Tremont, but Waddington didn't look around.

"Good morning, Captain. Beautiful sight, isn't it?"

"Yes, sir, it is. I didn't see much in this country when I first came out after the war but, well, it tends to grow on a body."

"Yes," Waddington said. "You learn to love it after a while. You want more of it and more of the freedom it offers." Waddington looked around at Tremont.

"I know your feelings about the Indians, sir, and, uh, well, I guess I kind of agree with you but—"

"But it's our land, isn't it, Captain? The land of white men?"

"That's what they're sayin' back in Washington."

"Yes. What's that noble term they're throwing around in the newspapers back East? Manifest destiny? That's a hell of a lofty title for piracy and murder, don't you agree, Captain?"

"Isn't that a little strong, sir? After all, we have tried to negotiate with the Indians."

"Tried? My god, man, we've signed more treaties with the Indian than you could carry in an Army ambulance. And every one of them has been a lie. Most were broken before the ink dried. Then, when they defend what was theirs in the first place, we scream savagery."

"No nation in history has ever progressed without war, sir."

"This isn't war, Captain. This is exactly what our forefathers fought against at Lexington and Concord." Waddington's face wrinkled and he rubbed his chin whiskers. "It sickens me, Captain. We're destroying an entire civilization, a race of people from whom we could learn how to live on the land. Mark my words, one day we'll destroy the land itself. And if we can figure out a way to do it, even the air."

Sergeant Mayhew suddenly appeared atop the ridge. He was holding a dispatch out toward Waddington.

"The rider you ordered out to Fort Robinson, sir. He's back."

"Good, good. Now maybe we can find out what the

hell is going on around here." Waddington opened the dispatch case and read:

> William Gunnison believed killed en route to Fort Randall. Crow scouts indicate Hunkpatila Sioux uprising along the Rosebud. Treaty talk with Red Cloud broken down. Col. Herschel Tubbs now moving north from the Platte to suspected area of Hunkpatila village. Urge support attack from the east in four days.
>
> A. Terry<br>General Comnd<br>Fort Robinson

"Four days?" Major Waddington looked at Sergeant Mayhew.

"That'd have to be tomorrow, sir. That dispatch rider figured a two-day ride to Randall, but he lost one day hightailin' it away from some Crow."

"We can't attack tomorrow, sir," Captain Tremont said. "Our other troops from the fort won't be here for another full day."

"Then we'll have to go without them. You stay here and bring them in for support as soon as you can."

"Yes, sir. I'll ride down and inform Lieutenant Boyer of the situation. My suggestion is that he move the wagons out at once."

"I agree," Waddington said. He glanced again at the dispatch and shook his head. "Gunnison," he mumbled thoughtfully, then repeated, "Gunnison." He was trying to place the name.

"He was knowed better as Gunn," Sergeant Mayhew said. "Damn good man, never seen anyone faster with a handgun, or more reluctant to use it. Didn't like to right 'less he was pushed into it, then look out. Oncet seen him take out three men down at Fort Kearny."

"I remember him now," Waddington said. "He rode some with Quantrill if I recollect. But he scouted for me some down on the Republican. He was a good man."

"No, he weren't never with Quantrill. Don't seem likely him gettin' killed this way," Mayhew observed.

"Yes, well, it's too bad about that. But right now we got other things to worry about. Like hopin' the Crow don't suddenly decide to join up with the Sioux."

"Not likely, Major," Sergeant Mayhew said. "Crow and Sioux don't mix too good. Still, could be. Could be." He turned and walked back down the hill and Waddington watched him leave. In fact, Waddington knew that the Sioux alone represented as formidable an enemy as the Army could handle, just then.

The wagons were finally formed and Major Waddington ordered his troops to break camp. As soon as the train was out of sight, he'd march his troopers west. He would be glad when both elements were in the field. Just at that moment, the entire gathering, large as it was, was at its most vulnerable.

Below the westward side of the slope on which Major Waddington had camped, out of sight of both the wagon train and the Army, Sinte Galeshka, Crippled Antelope and Kicking Bear also knew when the whites were most vulnerable. They had been there since before daylight. Kicking Bear and his Oglala Hunkpatila would ride north in a semicircle and strike the wagon train. When the troopers on the ridge started down to assist the train, Crippled Antelope's warriors would ride up the slope and strike from the rear. Sinte Galeshka would then ride close to the base of the ridge and strike the soldiers as they were driven downward. To ensure the success of the plan, Crippled Antelope had sent a dozen warriors along the opposite side of the river to draw the attention of both the soldiers with the wagon train and those on the ridge. Now, they struck.

"Sound the charge!" Waddington yelled.

Half-dressed troopers scrambled for stacked weapons. Below, Lieutenant Boyer ordered the wagons to form circles, but the Indians had waited until they were well strung out, and such a maneuver now would be difficult.

Half a dozen soldiers rushed to gather and hold the mounts in groups. They were cut down almost instantly. The proud cavalry would fight this day on foot. Even as the warriors across the river drew the fire of the wagon train guard, Kicking Bear ordered his first attack. Atop the ridge, Major Waddington winced as he saw the dust cloud stirred by 150 screaming Sioux.

Gunn knew he couldn't just stand by and do nothing. He was shirtless and the Sioux maidens had painted his body with the markings of a warrior. If he made it to the wagon train, he fully expected to be cut down, but he knew he'd have to try.

"Now, white eyes, we will see if you pass the test of Crippled Antelope." The big warrior lowered his raised arm and the Sioux started up the slope. That was when

Gunn made his move.

"Sorry, brother," he said. He knocked Crippled Antelope from his mount, hunkered down against his own horse and rode, hell-bent, toward Kicking Bear's position. Crippled Antelope glanced after him, but he couldn't take the time for revenge now. That would come later—if Gunn lived out the day.

Major Waddington's men were thrown into a rout. They fought in a disorganized array of groups and individuals, merely trying to survive. Sergeant Mayhew managed to pull together about thirty of them, two-thirds of the way down the slope. Suddenly, he found himself facing another group of antagonists, when Sinte Galeshka began his attack from the base of the slope.

Wagon after wagon erupted into flame as Kicking Bear's Sioux attacked, struck, withdrew and attacked again. Lieutenant Boyer stood with twenty troopers at the outset. Soon there were twelve, then eight. He fell back. Now, soldiers and the men and women of the wagon train fought side by side.

In the melee, Gunn had managed to ride in with one attacking wave of Sioux, then leap from his mount. He bellied along the ground and took cover in some reeds along the river. He realized he was nearly at the front end of the wagon train. Still, he was without a weapon.

Another attack came and this time, Sioux broke the half circle of wagons. Now, men fought hand-to-hand and Gunn could hear the screams of women and children. Suddenly, two wagons broke the circle, their horses whinnying and pulling hard in the soft ground. Then they were moving full speed. Gunn could see a man on the seat of the first. A Sioux warrior ventured parallel to the wagon. The rider leaped from his mount. The brave and the white man struggled.

Gunn got to his feet. Something rustled behind him. He whirled and saw a young soldier. The soldier's rifle was raised, but his mouth dropped open when he saw the color of Gunn's skin. Gunn moved, tackling him and putting him out cold with a solid punch. At the same time he heard the rending of metal and wood as the first wagon jackknifed and overturned. He could also hear the screams of children from inside.

Gunn grabbed the soldier's Springfield and checked it for a load. The second wagon was bearing down on him. Two Sioux were in hot pursuit. Gunn saw the driver, a woman — no, a girl, young, pretty, and with a look of controlled fear on her face.

Gunn aimed and fired. A warrior flew from his horse. Gunn grabbed the rear of the wagon and pulled hard. His feet scraped along the sandy ground and then his strength prevailed. He hauled himself into the wagon.

The girl screamed and Gunn could see the form of an Indian silhouetted against the canvas of the wagon. He'd lost the rifle, so he tried to get his balance and move forward. Suddenly there was a shot and the Indian flew off to the rear. Gunn saw a pistol in the girl's hand.

"Allow me, ma'am," Gunn said. He took the reins as the girl stared in awe at the whiteness of his skin, partially covered with the red, yellow and black of the war paint. "Don't ask any questions right now, miss. Just hang on," he said.

Gunn looked ahead. The river took a sharp bend and the wagon was bearing down fast on a bluff. He knew there was no time to turn it. At the last possible moment, Gunn grabbed the girl by the waist and pushed off, hard, with both legs. They flew into the air, out . . . out, down, down, and then the dark and blood-roiled waters of the Rosebud closed around them.

## Chapter Eleven

Gunn ached in every muscle and joint.

The bruise on his forehead had turned to a lump of pain and the sharp, stabbing pains on his left side could have been because of a broken rib. He eased himself up to his hands and knees and shook off a wave of nausea. He coughed and it was like the blow of a sledgehammer in his side. Slowly, he got to his feet.

"The girl," Gunn said aloud. He stood up and looked around for her. He had no idea how far downstream they had been carried, but where they hit the water the current had been strong and the water deep.

Gunn remembered the big rock. It had loomed just ahead of them and he had used his own body to shield the girl's. He must have lost his grip on her then. He struck the rock hard, and after that, everything was blurry.

It was still daylight, though the sun was low and he was in a huge stand of trees which almost blotted out the sky. Gunn finally got his bearings, then decided to walk upstream. He didn't have to go far, twenty or thirty yards at most, before he saw her. A crumpled heap, her feet still in the water. He hurried over to her, then knelt beside her. She was alive.

It took him the better part of half an hour, but Gunn finally got a small fire going, well away from the river. The girl was fully awake now, and in better shape than he was. He looked toward her.

"You come any closer, mister, and I'll put a hole clean through you."

"You still have the pistol?"

For answer, the girl cocked it, and he heard the click of the turning cylinder. She was sitting just outside the fringe of light from the fire. He could see her form, but not her features. He realized that she'd seen him half-naked and painted up like a savage. Even the dousing in the river hadn't removed all the paint.

"I won't do you any harm," he said.

"You sure as hell won't, you half-breed bastard," the girl said.

"Move by the fire. Dry yourself," Gunn said.

"I'm fine, right where I am. You just stay right there where I can see you." He could see the pistol now.

"Is it still loaded?"

"You want to try me?"

Gunn remembered her shooting the Indian off the wagon. She had been calm then, very calm. He figured that if the pistol really was loaded, she could handle herself now if she thought she had to. He stayed just where she told him, squatting by the fire Indian-fashion, to warm himself.

"You saved my skin today, but don't get any ideas that I owe you anything," the girl said. "I been handlin' myself all right for quite a spell."

"I don't doubt that," Gunn said. "But, like I told you, you don't have to worry about me."

"I'm not worried about you, mister. And I intend to keep it that way."

"Look, lady, we can't stay here. I don't know how that fight came out, but right now there's a good a chance as any we'll be spotted by Indians as well as by whites. Better, maybe. Soon as we get dry, we'd best move east."

"We aren't goin' anywhere, mister," the girl said. "Come daylight, I'll figure out what to do." Something wet and stringy hit Gunn in the face. It was a length of corset tie. "Lash your ankles together, tight now. Then lie down and roll over on your stomach."

The girl punctuated her demand by pointing the pistol at Gunn's head. She was either the best damned bluffer Gunn had ever run up against, or she'd damn sure kill him. He complied. A moment later, she finished the job by tying his wrists behind him.

Though Gunn had asked her no questions, the girl seemed to feel a need to talk, to tell her story. "The name's Lisa Briggs," she said. He could hear the rustle of her dress which had partially dried. He twisted his head to the side and caught the glimpse of a gleaming thigh. She was stripped down to the loosened corset. "Got no kin left. My little brother died of the fever last winter in St. Joe, waitin' for spring and this God-awful trip. Folks died in a fire back east, three years ago. I've been livin' with my aunt and uncle. They're the ones brought me out here."

"Where are they?"

"Back at that camp. They died in the first attack."

Lisa had stood before the fire naked, drying her petticoat. Gunn could see the softness of one of her breasts, its pink tip hardened by the cool night air. She slipped the petticoat over her head and then held out the dress. It was lavender and lacy. Gunn wondered about her choice of wardrobe on that day, then concluded it was done in anticipation of reaching Fort Randall before nightfall.

"Look, miss. I'm not what you think I am," Gunn said.

"Maybe. Maybe not. I don't really give a damn who or what you are. You saved my life and that'll probably save yours. We'll see, come morning. Good night, mister."


The pain in Gunn's side suddenly increased and the air gushed out of his lungs. He groaned and his head was jerked back by a meaty hand gripping a handful of his hair.

"Why does the white eye wear the paint of a Hunkpatila warrior?" The hand released his hair and grabbed an arm, rolling him onto his back. Gunn was looking into the face of a Crow warrior. He'd never heard them. He glanced past the warrior and saw two more. Between them, bound and gagged, was Lisa Briggs.

"I was a prisoner, but I escaped from the Hunkpatila," he said.

The Crow kneeling beside him got him to his feet. One of the others approached him.

"You will not run away from the Crow. We are not old women like the Hunkpatila. You will see me take your woman before I cut out your heart." The warrior backhanded Gunn, and with his ankles still tied, he couldn't keep his balance. He went down like a sack of lead. He didn't get to his feet again until the Indians dragged him up, cut the tie on his ankles, then made him get on a horse. The horses, Gunn noted, bore the markings of U.S. Cavalry.

They rode south and east, nearly the same route Gunn had been following when he'd seen the buffalo herd. One of the Crow rode ahead, while the others were just behind. Gunn finally managed to ease his mount alongside the girl.

"Did they get that little handgun of yours?" he whispered. She neither answered nor looked toward him. "Damn it, girl," he hissed. "Whatever you think I am, I'm sure as hell no Crow!"

"They didn't get it," she replied. Then she turned and looked at him. "And neither will you."

"Do not speak to the Hunkpatila white dog," one of the Crow said. He jammed his rifle butt into Gunn's back, and Gunn's mount broke into a trot, pulling him ahead of Lisa Briggs.

Gunn snorted at his own situation. He was a white man, painted up like a Sioux, the captive of Indians who hated both Sioux and whites with equal passion, and in the company of a white woman who hated him just as much. It was, in Gunn's mind, another one-word situation.

"Shit," he mumbled.

## Chapter Twelve

Major Waddington removed his glasses, squeezed the bridge of his nose and rubbed his eyes. He looked up and saw his wife.

"Coffee, Josiah?"

"I'd rather have whiskey."

She nodded, and a moment later returned, bringing with her a bottle and two glasses.

"You're going to join me, Ellie?"

"Yes," Ellie said. "My father approved of liquor for medicinal purposes. I consider this very medicinal."

"Young Boyer. Did you look in on him, Ellie?"

"Yes. I'm afraid all we can do is pray for his life. The doctor said his leg was going to have to be amputated."

"God," Josiah sighed. "He's so young. He was so confident, so proud."

"What happened, Josiah? Do you want to talk about it now?"

"Talk about it? What's there to talk about, Ellie? I lost nearly an entire company out there. Fought it like—well, like I would have thought Lieutenant Boyer would have done. I was a fool. I know the enemy better than that."

"You mustn't blame yourself, Josiah. From what Sergeant Mayhew told me, it's very fortunate any of you returned."

"You know I've got to get back, don't you? This time with a full regiment. The Hunkpatila must be broken, once and for all."

"I know, Josiah, but—"

"But if I'm court-martialed in St. Louis, I'll not have to go. Is that it, Ellie?"

"Isn't life more precious than anything?"

"Is it? Life with a husband who has been drummed out of the Army because he led his command to slaughter. Is that more precious?"

"But you don't know that's what they'll do. Other officers have suffered defeat. Many of them."

"Not the ones with my experience. Men like young Boyer, maybe, or even Captain Tremont." Waddington shook his head in disbelief. "You should have seen him, Ellie. Tremont. God! He lined his men up like rows of corn and the Sioux cut him down like a sapling. I screamed at him, I tried to rally the others but . . ." Ellie Waddington could see the tears in her husband's eyes and she moved to comfort him.

The fight on the Rosebud had been bloody. Forty-eight troopers died, seventeen more critically wounded. Eight children, six women and nine men died in the wagon train. Several people, both Army and civilian, were still unaccounted for, among them, a young white girl named Lisa Briggs.

The door to the Waddington's living room burst

open and Sergeant Mayhew hurried in. He was holding up a dispatch and smiling broadly.

"Don't mean to be showin' my bad manners, sir, but I had to come tell you. General Terry got whupped too. Red Cloud's Oglala sent 'em packin' back to Robinson. His report to St. Louis give you the credit fer savin' his hide. He tol' 'em if'n it hadn't been for you holdin' off the Hunkpatila, he'd a prob'ly got massacred."

"Let me see that, Sergeant," Waddington said, slipping his glasses on, carefully hooking them over each ear. He read it quickly, then handed it to his wife. "They're sending five new troops."

"Yes, sir, and they're sendin' 'em here. You'll be commandin' 'em, Colonel."

"Colonel?"

"I was talkin' to Josh Tapley. He said they weren't no way you'd have command of that many men 'n' not be a colonel."

"Josiah, it says here the men are experienced Indian fighters," Ellie said.

"Yes'm," Mayhew said. "They been fightin' Cheyenne down south, and afore that, Apache. We git them fellas in here, we'll run them Sioux clean to the big mountains."

"It's hard to believe," Waddington said. "Terry! Damn, I never got along particularly well with him, Ellie, but I always did believe he was a fair man."

"He certainly proved it by this, Josiah. A lesser man might have blamed his defeat on you."

"Yes. You're right." Waddington walked over to Sergeant Mayhew and put his hands on his shoulder. "Sergeant, I think this command is big enough for a sergeant-major now, and I want you to handle that job for me."

Mayhew grinned broadly. "Never figured on keepin' what I got this long, let alone makin' sergeant-major," he said.

"You've earned it, Sergeant-Major. And I need someone I can count on out there."

"Well, if'n you order it, sir, I reckon I'll do it."

"I'm not ordering it. I'm asking it, one old campaigner to another, one old friend to another."

"Then I reckon I'll do it. Them devils whupped us good this time, but I reckon they won't be doin' it again," Mayhew said.

"No, not again." Waddington turned away and walked over to his desk. He rubbed his chin whiskers, glanced at his wife and then turned back to the sergeant. "Do you want to know why we got whipped? We went out for the wrong reasons, and probably for the wrong Indians. Now, of course, we've got to fight the Hunkpatila but we'll be smart about it. We'll arrange for a movement of the tribe to a reservation. We'll talk to them, give them a chance. We'll fight only if we have to."

"Yes, sir. I believe that there is the way to do it."

"And we'll begin at once. We don't need five new troops of cavalry to talk, do we, Sergeant-Major?"

"No, sir. But we'll have to find somebody that can get us with them Hunkpatila. Don't figure they'll just let us ride in."

Waddington laughed for the first time in several days. "No, Sergeant-Major. I don't reckon they will." He rubbed his chin whiskers again, pacing a few feet in each direction. Suddenly he looked up. "Get me Seth Kincaid. I believe he's down at Fort Kearny."

"Yes, sir, that's what I heard."

"Get him."


Far to the west, where the Rosebud gains water from Hanging Woman creek, a great council fire burned. Around it, passing the smoke pipe of victory, sat Sinte Galeshka, Kicking Bear, Short Bull, Kicking Bird, American Horse and Red Cloud. It was Red Cloud who spoke first.

"We have sent the Blue Coats back to their forts soaked in their own blood. It is because of this thing I have called for the council."

"Should not the young men sit with us?" Kicking Bear asked. "They have taken many coups."

"No. What we shall speak of is for men who are old and wise, not men who are young and full of hot blood. I have heard from Ten Bears, Lone Wolf and Roman Nose."

"They are Crow, Cheyenne and Comanche. They are enemies of the Sioux," Sinte Galeshka said.

Red Cloud held up his arm. "It was so, Sinte Galeshka. But now they wish to be our brothers."

"How can enemies fight as brothers?"

"Don't all white men now fight as brothers? And didn't they once fight a great war where some wore blue and some wore gray?"

"That is true."

"And does the white soldier not fight alongside the buffalo soldiers of black skin?"

"That is also true."

"Then hear me. I say we can learn a lesson from the whites."

"But the Hunkpatila have taken many coups from the Crow. And the Crow have killed many Lakota."

"But each, the Crow, the Lakota, the Comanche and the Cheyenne, have taken many coups from the Blue Coats. Could not many more be taken if we fought as brothers?"

"We must talk of this," Short Bull said. "I think many of the young men will not see this."

"There is no time for talk," Red Cloud replied. "There is only time for deeds. We must join together and fight together, now."

"We cannot fight together if we do not speak of this."

"Each of the chiefs has already spoken. They will bring together their warriors with our warriors. We will lead all the young men against a Blue Coat fort. We have chosen the fort on the Rosebud, the one the pony soldiers call Randall. When the young men see that, together, we are stronger even than the white man's fort, they will know that this is the right thing to do."

Red Cloud's plan didn't go down all that easily. The others talked among themselves, voices lifted and lowered as the chiefs debated and discussed the plan. No such thing had been done since many years before when the forts were small and weakly defended. Finally, Sinte Galeshka spoke.

"In one more moon, Red Cloud, bring together the Oglala and the Teton. Bring together the warriors of Ten Bears, Lone Wolf and Roman Nose. We, too, will come, the Hunkpatila of Kicking Bear and Sinte

Galeshka. We will come and gather at the sacred burial ground of our fathers."

"The creek called Wounded Knee."

"It is so. From there, together, we will drive the pony soldiers from the fort on the Rosebud."

## Chapter Thirteen

Gunn had feigned sleep long enough that morning to have overheard the three Crow warriors. While he'd missed several words, he was able to put together that they were outcasts from their own village. There was talk of the Crow joining the Sioux and these three wanted no part of it. Apparently there were others like them, forty or fifty perhaps. Gunn knew that he and Lisa Briggs would have no time left if they were taken to the meeting place.

"My Sioux brothers told me the Crow were old women. Now I know why they said this thing." Gunn swallowed hard. He'd committed himself to his plan but rogue Indians didn't have to play by the rules.

"Have you decided this is a good day to die?"

"At the hands of old women? I killed the sacred white buffalo," Gunn said. He touched his chin to his chest, indicating the necklace he wore. The Crow studied it and Gunn could see by his expression that the Crow knew this was sacred.

"You are a white man. You have stolen the spirit of

the white buffalo from the dead body of a Crow."

"I couldn't steal this from a Crow. No Crow could kill a white buffalo."

"I can cut out your tongue, white man, then you will speak no more of the Crow."

"And who will you tell of this?" Gunn asked. He dropped to his knees, bowed his head and shook the buffalo bone which hung from around his neck. After a few moments he stood and smiled. "There is no one you can tell because you are an outcast, you and your brothers. You have no chief, no tribe, no village and no women."

"How do you know these things?"

"The white buffalo spirit gives me the power to see and Tatanka Wakan, the Great Spirit of all Indians, whispers to me on the wind."

"I do not believe you."

"Then put me to the test. Set my woman and me free, then follow us. If you can kill me, you can have my woman and the spirit of the sacred buffalo." Gunn walked back to Lisa Briggs and stood there watching the Indians discuss his proposition.

"What are you trying to do?" Lisa hissed.

"Get us out of here," Gunn said.

"By trading me?"

"Believe me, miss, if we wait until they join the others, you'll need that pistol for yourself."

Lisa looked into Gunn's eyes and knew he wasn't kidding. She couldn't quite figure him out and she didn't trust him. Still . . . there was something about him.

The biggest Crow walked toward them.

"Keep quiet," he said to Lisa. "No matter what

happens, keep quiet!"

The Crow took his hunting knife and freed both of them from their bonds, then he stepped back and looked at the sun. He bent over and thrust his knife into the ground. The shadow was short. Gunn estimated it was ten-thirty, perhaps eleven o'clock. He knew what was coming.

"When the knife makes no more shadow, we will follow and test you. Go!"

They were barely out of sight when Gunn grabbed Lisa's arm. "We've got an hour and a half at most."

"They've got horses, we haven't. Did you think about that?"

"You got a better idea, I'll listen," Gunn said. She didn't. "You can give me that pistol or I can take it away from you, but it's all we've got between us and these three."

"I've only got five bullets for it."

"Then I'll have to make every one of them count, won't I?"

"Who are you, mister?"

Gunn smirked. "You pick a lousy time to get acquainted," he said. "I'll be glad to fill you in on the details, Miss Briggs, some other time. Now, how about that pistol?"

Lisa raised her dress, high. Gunn saw a flash of creamy thigh. She removed the small pistol from a garter holster.

"You really think hiding that pistol there would stop a man from taking it away from you?"

Now it was Lisa's turn to smile. "No," she said. "But it's proven a good way to distract their attention long enough for me to blow a hole in 'em."

"I'll try to remember that," Gunn said. He looked back toward where they had left the Crow and then in the opposite direction. He pointed toward a stand of trees about half a mile from the river. "Get up to those trees and wait."

"For what?"

"For me, Miss Briggs."

"And if you don't show up?"

"Then you'll have Crow for company." Gunn eyed the little pistol with contempt. It wasn't his Colt, but he had seen it kill an Indian. In any event, it was all he had.

Gunn worked his way back east and then down along a ridge which horseshoed around the spot where they had camped. It took him about fifteen minutes to get into a position where he could see the Crow. He glanced up at the sun. It seemed higher than he thought. Maybe he'd figured the time too tight.

Two of the Indians were squatting near where the fire had been. The third one, the big Crow warrior, stood near the horses. He was looking off in the direction Gunn and Lisa had taken. Gunn edged along the trees, crouching low, thankful there was no breeze. He hoped the horses wouldn't hear him. Finally he was as close as he felt he could get. He squatted down and checked the pistol.

"Whoeee, whoee." The sound was soft, audible, he hoped, only to the nearest Crow. It was a Sioux signal. The Crow reacted by moving a few feet closer. He was carrying a rifle and Gunn saw him bring the hammer back on the Springfield. Gunn found a piece of tree limb. He picked it up. Carefully, he drew back his arm and tossed it to the right. The Crow raised his rifle and

Gunn made his move. He fired with deadly aim. The shot was accurate and fatal.

Gunn reached the dead Crow, grabbed the rifle and cursed beneath his breath because the horses bolted. The first of the other warriors to come in sight was the only other one with a rifle. Gunn steadied the Springfield, waited, then fired. The Crow dropped, a bullet through his forehead.

"Over here, you big son of a bitch!" Gunn called to the last one. "Come get me."

The third Crow unsheathed his knife, let out a war whoop and ran, full bore, toward Gunn. He knew Gunn's rifle was empty and he smiled in triumph as he closed the distance.

Gunn waited until the Indian was right on him, then he raised the little pistol the Indian hadn't seen. Gunn dropped him with one shot and the fight was over.

Gunn climbed the ridge and made a cursory search for the horses, but they were gone. On foot, he returned to Lisa Briggs.

"We'd best move," he said. "We've got a long walk ahead of us."

"The pistol," Lisa said, holding out her hand.

"You mean I still haven't earned your trust?"

"The pistol, mister. I want it back, now!"

Gunn shrugged and gave it to her.

"I only had to use two bullets."

"Yes, but you didn't get us a horse, did you?" Lisa slipped the little gun back into its holster, straightened her dress, then looked back at Gunn. "Which way?"

"East, toward Fort Randall. If we get lucky, we'll run into an Army patrol." Gunn was about to tell her who he was when he noticed the strange look on her face.

She paled somewhat and her eyes were now focused just over his left shoulder. "Lisa?"

She didn't respond.

Gunn turned. There, emerging from a dry creek bed, was Crippled Antelope and a dozen Sioux warriors.

# Chapter Fourteen

Seth Kincaid resembled an old grizzly bear. His huge shoulders rounded down from a bull neck and flowed into giant arms. Seth had spent his younger years swilling free whiskey by virtue of being able to hoist a Conestoga wagon wheel over his head with just one of those arms. Adding to his bulk was an outsized buckskin jacket and britches. Those he held up with a thickly woven belt of black braids which, according to Seth, came from a mixture of "Injuns." No one seemed anxious to dispute him.

Sergeant-Major Mayhew telegraphed Fort Kearny and learned that Seth was headed west. He caught up with the old scout at a way station in Gothenburg, Nebraska Territory. Seth listened, and agreed to return to Fort Randall.

"I assume Sergeant-Major Mayhew told you what I want to do," Waddington said. True to Josh Tapley's prediction, Mayhew's promotion to colonel had come through and the leaves glistened brightly from the weathered cavalry-yellow field of his shoulder boards.

"What do you want to pen the Sioux up like a herd of cattle for?" Seth asked. He spit toward the spittoon.

"So they will survive, Mister Kinkaid, so they will survive." Colonel Waddington lit his pipe and walked over to the window to look out over the dry parade ground. He saw the guard leaning against the wall of the sallyport and made a mental note to speak with the officer-of-the-day.

"Ever ask 'em if they want to survive?" Kinkaid asked.

"Of course they want to survive, sir."

"No, they don't. Not if it means they got to survive on a reservation. You do better by 'em when you fight 'em, let 'em get in a lick or two, then finish 'em off. They's a proud lot, the Sioux. Same be for the rest of 'em. The Cheyenne, Comanch', even the Apache."

"We're a Christian civilization, Mister Kinkaid," the colonel said. He lit his pipe and took several deep draws to keep it going, sending up a cloud of blue smoke. "We're not all good, and we're not always right but, in the scheme of things, I have to think that God has planned for both the white man and the red."

"Yes, sir, Colonel," Seth answered. "I kin agree with that, s'long as it ain't the same place."

"I don't quite understand you, Kinkaid. I'm sympathetic to the plight of the Indian, but I'm also a practical man. Now you, well, I've heard you're sympathetic to them as well, but you seem to have spent more time killing than helping then."

"If'n a man come to me an' said, 'Mister Kinkaid, I'm wantin' to help you, so I'm gonna keep you from the mountains and the streams and your trappin' and roamin' country. But don't you worry none 'cause I plan to give you ever'thing I think you need,' I reckon I'd have to ask him one question."

"And what would that be?"

"If'n I don't want the help, what then? If'n his answer is that I take his help or he'll have to kill me, I reckon I'd tell him to get to killin'."

"Yes. I agree. Only recently I told Mayhew here that the Indian was doing nothing more than our own forefathers did against the British less than a hundred years ago. But—"Waddington sighed—"well, hell, this is different."

Seth's face broke into a broad grin. "I recollect hearin' somethin' like that out of one of them Englishmen come out on the Platte to hunt. He said that if'n the British was still here, the whole country'd be civilized now. But us, colonials, he called us, we was different, he said."

Colonel Waddington had been on that very hunting trip and he felt his face flushing with the memory of it. It was time to end the discussion.

"I want you to set up a meeting with the Hunkpatila. How long will it take, Kinkaid?"

"Which tribe?"

"Both. Who are the chiefs?"

"Sinte Galeshka's one of 'em an' the other one's name is Kicking Bear." Seth pointed a thick, gnarled finger at the colonel. "Done a heap o' scoutin' for the Army, set up a heap o' councils with the Injuns. But I'll tell you, Colonel, I won't stand fer no lyin' to 'em. I won't sit with you, and I won't put my name to paper. Won't back nothin' you tell 'em. That there is on yore head."

"I understand that, Kinkaid. But will you help round them up if they agree to move onto a reservation?"

Seth grinned his toothless grin again. "Would, Colonel, 'ceptin' for one thing."

"What's that?"

"I'll be too busy killin' them what won't go."

Waddington nodded weakly.

"When can we leave?" he asked.

"Sunup tomorry's fine by me. You bring ol' Mayhew here an' a dozen troopers. Good ones, mind you, but no more than that."

"Do you know where they are? Exactly, I mean?"

"Never know where a Sioux is, 'xactly, Colonel, less'n he wants you to know, or it's too late." Seth walked to the door and then turned back, grinning again. "I figure if'n we look hard enough, Colonel, them Hunkpatila's bound to find us."

By Gunn's reckoning, two factors had prevented Crippled Antelope from finishing him off right on the spot. First was the fact that Gunn, somehow, had survived the fight on the Rosebud, even unarmed. Crippled Antelope could not discount the spirit of the white buffalo in protecting him. The second was Lisa Briggs. In her, perhaps, the angered Sioux warrior could mete out an even more painful revenge against Gunn.

Back in the village of Sinte Galeshka, Crippled Antelope quickly separated Gunn and Lisa. Gunn summoned Crow King.

"She's my woman," he said. "By your law."

"It is for Sinte Galeshka to decide."

"Then take me to him."

"He has ridden to the hills to hear the words of Tatanka Wakan and bring back strong medicine for the sacred meeting."

"Sacred meeting? What meeting?"

"Soon, Shadow Hand, the Hunkpatila will ride against the Blue Coat fort called Randall. They will ride with their brothers, the Oglala of Red Cloud and the Cheyenne, Crow and Comanche."

Gunn winced. "How soon?"

"Before another moon. We will gather with our brothers on the sacred burial ground and drive the Blue Coats out of our land. Then it will be ours forever."

"Fort Randall is only one fort, Crow King. Even together there aren't enough of you to wipe out all the forts."

"Last night, the Shaman read the bleached bones of the sacred buffalo again. It is there at the fort called Randall, where we must stop the Blue Coats. The Oglala of Red Cloud will kill all in the white man's wagons on the Platte and the Republican. The Hunkpatila will drive them from the Rosebud and with our brothers, we will ride to the Paha Sapa. No pony soldier can ride there."

"The woman," Gunn said. "Will she be safe?"

"I will keep her safe until the return of Sinte Galeshka."

Crow King left Gunn's tipi and, for the first time in days, the loner was once again alone. Gunn rolled a smoke, lit it and took a deep pull. He exhaled slowly and watched the smoke curl upward, then fan out as a slight breeze slipped through the opening.

Crow King's news had not come as a complete surprise. There had been rumors for months about a gathering of all the tribes. Now, that seemed a reality.

Gunn shuddered at the prospect. No creek, no

stream, no river would be free of the flow of human blood. There would be no battle lines and no quarter would be asked or given.

The buffalo-hide door rustled. Gunn looked up and saw the silhouette of a woman. It was Lisa Briggs. The women had dressed her in bleached buckskins. They were new, tight and molded to her lithe, young body.

"Come in," Gunn said quietly.

"I'm here because they forced me to be. I'm to stay here tonight. You are to go to the chief's lodge. Some spirit or something is supposed to sleep with me tonight, then they'll know who I belong to."

"It's just Sioux superstition. You won't be harmed."

"And I won't belong to anybody unless I say so."

"Don't be a fool, girl. You try anything here and we'll both lose our hair. Or worse." Gunn crushed out his smoke and walked over to Lisa. She drew back, moving around him.

"I was beginning—" she paused—"I mean, I thought you might be something after all. But now . . ."

"Look, Lisa, it's a long story."

"Well, don't waste it on me," Lisa said. "Just get out."

"For now, lady, that'll have to do," Gunn agreed.

# Chapter Fifteen

Gunn got a shock when he entered Sinte Galeshka's tipi on the morning of the third day after the old chief's return from the hills. Sinte Galeshka handed Gunn his clothes and his Colt.

"I'm free to go?"

"At the white man's trading post on the big river you will meet two men. You will give them this." He handed Gunn a canvas poke. It was heavy and Gunn looked inside.

"Gold?" he said.

"Yes. You give them gold, they will give you rifles—rifles that shoot many times like this one." He picked up Gunn's Winchester.

"Repeating rifles? No." Gunn tossed the little sack of gold down. "Men who sell guns to Indians are bad business for everyone. Get yourself another man. I won't do it."

"Then the white woman will belong to Crippled Antelope."

"That's blackmail." Gunn saw that the warrior did not understand. "You trade with threats and force, not with goods."

"I have no wish to blackmail," Sinte Galeshka said. "I thought you would do it without force."

"What made you think that? Anyway, why would you want me to?"

"You would know if the guns are good."

"And with these guns you would ride against Fort Randall?" Gunn asked.

"Yes. But do not worry. We will not ask you to go. Return with the guns and you may claim your woman and ride free."

Gunn thought about it. He couldn't let Lisa fall into Crippled Antelope's hands. On the other hand, he couldn't be a party to this—unless, somehow, he could use it to get word to Waddington of the impending attack.

"All right, Sinte Galeshka, I'll do it. But I go alone and it'll take me about three days. I know a little something about gun runners and I want to check these two out before I approach them."

"Crow King will go with you."

"Only to a mile or so away from the post, then he must wait for me. This is my kind of business, and I'll do it my way."

"Very well, Shadow Hand. You shall do it the way you wish. Leave tomorrow night."

"I'll leave now. I'll be at the trading post in the morning. Who are these two men?"

"One has an eye that cannot see, the other has a scar, here." Sinte Galeshka made the mark of a scar on his cheek.

"Will and Clay Lassiter," Gunn said. "How the hell did you ever get hooked up with them?"

"I don't understand."

"Never mind. They're a couple of hardcases, that's for sure. How about my rifle?"

"You need only the pistol, Shadow Hand. I have seen its medicine."

"Yeah, I guess you have."

As Gunn hurried across the village circle to his own tipi, he saw Bright Moon just coming out.

"This is the woman you have chosen, Shadow Hand?" she asked.

"I wouldn't exactly put it that way," he said, adding, "and I don't think she'd even come close."

"Did you not save her for yourself?"

"I saved her, Bright Moon. For what, exactly, I'm not yet sure."

"When you return, I will come to you and you will choose," Bright Moon said. It was the last kind of trouble Gunn needed then, but he nodded. He slipped into the tipi and found no one else there but Lisa.

"You've got a gun. Are we free?"

"No, we're not. I've got to ride to Barker's Trading Post and make a deal for the Sioux. If I don't, Sinte Galeshka will give you to Crippled Antelope, that big warrior who brought us back. If I make it, you'll be fine."

"Who are you? What are you?" Lisa asked.

Gunn shook his head. It seemed there was never the time to finally tell Lisa what he was all about. "I'll explain that too, Lisa, when I get back. Three days if it goes well. Stay out of trouble."

The Sioux let Gunn ride Esquire so that, with his own clothes, pistol and horse under him, he felt like himself for the first time since he had been captured. Of course there was a big Indian riding alongside, keeping an eye on him. That didn't bother him, he knew he could get away from Crow King anytime he wanted, probably without having to kill him, which he didn't really want to do. But it would do no good, for as long as Lisa was a prisoner back in the village, he was as confined as if he were tied with the best hemp rope.

Barker's Trading Post was more than a trading post but less than a town. Abe Barker had started with no more than a log house with a lean-to. Now it was about the only thing of substance between Omaha, the forts along the Platte and the French-German settlement at Fort Pierre. Old Abe was dead and gone now, but his two sons carried out his trade and traditions.

Gunn left Crow King in a stand of trees along the river and rode into the trading post alone. There was a single dirt road with a few buildings on each side. It covered about a block and a half. There were three saloons, two of them separate from the main trading post. There was a livery barn run by the blacksmith, and what passed for a rooming house. In fact, it was a brothel, perhaps the only brothel for two hundred miles in any direction.

"You lose somethin', mister?"

Gunn didn't answer. He let his eyes adjust from the bright sun to the semidarkness of Abe's saloon. There was no one in the place except the bartender and an old drunk, already passed out at a corner table. Gunn walked up to the bar.

"What'll you have?"

"Information, for now," Gunn said.

"I don't make money givin' out information."

"I'm looking for the Lassiters," Gunn said. He saw the bartender's expression perk up and knew that he had gotten his attention.

"What for you want 'em?"

"That's my business. You seen 'em?"

The man took his first good look at Gunn. He frowned. He couldn't recall the face, but it was obvious there was something familiar about it.

"I know you, mister?" he asked

"I doubt it. How about the Lassiters?"

"Haven't been in for quite a spell now," the bartender said. He busied himself wiping glasses. "But then, they don't come in here too often, anyways."

"Where do they go?"

"Mostly down to Selma Lee's place. Either the whore house or her saloon."

Gunn smiled. Selma Lee Fraser. She was still there. He remembered her from Omaha. Then, about a year back, Gunn had drifted into Barker's post and spent the night with her. The next morning he'd run up against a gunny name of Jake Braxton. Braxton had worked over one of Selma Lee's girls. Gunn planned to give him a dose of his own medicine but a six-gun got in the way. Gunn's Colt put Braxton up on the hill next to old Abe Barker.

Gunn tossed a coin on the bar. "Have one on me," he said. "For the information."

"Didn't give you none."

"Selma Lee will."

Gunn had to step aside to let another man get through the bat-wing doors. The man looked hard at Gunn but he couldn't place the face either. Gunn did. The man was Jason Barker, one of old Abe's sons.

There was a little more action at Selma's saloon. Four men, drovers from their looks, sat playing cards.

Two others stood at the bar, talking. This time Gunn asked for a drink. He downed the rye, then ordered another.

"I'm looking for the Lassiter brothers," Gunn said. He downed the second shot and looked at the bartender for any reaction.

"Don't know anyone by that name. Only been workin' here a week."

"Is Selma Lee around?"

"Who wants to know?"

"Just tell her she's got a Gunn waiting for her, one that still shoots straight."

"Hold on, mister."

Gunn raised his hand in a gesture of calm. "Just tell her, she'll understand. It's not what you think." The man shrugged and walked away, disappearing behind a curtain. He reappeared a moment later and motioned for Gunn.

Neither Gunn nor Selma said anything until the bartender was out of earshot, then Selma hoisted her right leg up and rested her foot on the back of a chair. Gunn eyed the bare leg and followed it to the shadowy recesses he remembered so well.

"It's been a long, dry spell," she said.

"Oh?" Gunn grinned. "You've been faithful to me then?"

Selma Lee laughed. "About as faithful as you've been, I'd wager," she said. She dropped her leg, straightened her robe and poured them both a drink. As she handed it to him, she leaned over and, showing a generous amount of cleavage, whispered, "I've got to confess, though, that the quality has dropped considerable."

"I'd like to correct that, Selma, but I can't. Not this trip."

"You got the law on you?"

"Something like that."

"Sheriff, U.S. Marshal or the Army. Which is it?"

"Sioux."

"Sioux? Good God almighty, Gunn, what the hell kind of mess are you in now?"

"It's a long story."

"Sad too, I'll bet."

Gunn grinned. "A little."

"And a squaw tossed in for good measure. You got some big Sioux buck on your ass and you're lookin' for a place to hole up."

"You got the facts all there," Gunn said. "Just a little out of order, that's all. I'm looking for the Lassiter brothers."

Selma's nonchalance disappeared, replaced by a look of concern.

"Jesus, Gunn, ain't you got trouble enough? I saw you take out Jake Braxton, and I remember the greased lightnin' hand in Omaha. But, Gunn, neither of them could stand up to Clay Lassiter." She turned away, poured herself another drink and downed it before she turned back. "An' then there's Will and that damn sawed-off he totes."

"I'm not lookin' to fight them, Selma. We've got sort of a deal cookin'."

"You dealin' with the likes o' the Lassiters? You're a damned liar, William Gunnison." Selma walked over to him and slipped her arms around his neck. Gunn could smell the scent of her, something no Indian woman possessed because of the animal fat that they ate, and used to cover their bodies. "Maybe you've changed," she whispered.

"I haven't," Gunn said, pulling away gently. "But I can't afford to get careless. Have you seen them?"

"They'll be here tomorrow,' she said.

Gunn drew a breath.

That would cut him short one day.

One day could be an eternity — and hell at the other end.

## Chapter Sixteen

As tempting as it had been, Gunn resisted the urge to spend the night with Selma Lee. Instead, he returned to the river and Crow King. The big warrior, normally alert to every new sound, every new scent, was not alert this morning. Gunn awakened himself, saddled Esquire, and was halfway down the hill to Barker's post before Crow King stirred.

"I'll be back," Gunn called.

Crow King frowned, but did not reply.

The sun was full up by the time Gunn reached the livery. It was already warm enough to stir the flies and Esquire's tail switched at them constantly as the big horse snorted his annoyance. Gunn paid the smithy, not wanting to take time later for such a detail. For one thing, he wasn't sure he'd have the time.

He left the livery and cut a diagonal path to the opposite side of the street. He'd have a better view of Selma Lee's place and maybe even spot two horses he hadn't seen before. There were no new ones at the livery. Either the Lassiters hadn't arrived yet, or they weren't planning to stay any longer than necessary.

Gunn passed the still-locked outer door of Abe's place and stopped. He looked back over his shoulder, then from door-to-door on the opposite side of the street. He bent slightly and tied down his holster. He adjusted it, hefted the Colt partially out of it, then made a fist several times with his right hand to limber his fingers. It had been a while.

Gunn was just reaching up to push open the door at Selma Lee's place. A board creaked off to his left. He whirled to face it.

"I saw you yesterday, mister. I'm Jace Barker. What you lookin' for?"

"Not what," Gunn answered. "Who. I'm waiting for the Lassiter brothers. You got any objections?"

"If you're plannin' to gun 'em down, yeah, I got an objection. I remember you gunnin' a man down here once before. He wasn't worth much, but a federal marshal showed up and started askin' a lot of questions. That's not good for business."

"I'm not here to gun them. We've got a business deal."

"I don't like the way the Lassiters do business. You want to meet 'em at Selma Lee's place, fine. But do your business outside the post."

"Is that by Selma's request?"

The man shook his head and jammed his index finger into his own chest. "It's mine and it's not a request. Selma's here because me an' my brother let her be. You do it our way or not at all." The man's feet shifted. They were wide apart. Gunn had to admire the man's spunk. "You got any objections?"

"None I can think of," Gunn said. "I'll just stay right here 'til they show up, then we'll all ride out together."

"I'll hold you to that, mister. Make sure it happens just that way."

Gunn sat down to a platter of steak and eggs. It was beef, not buffalo, and he was surprised. Selma joined him for coffee.

"How'd you manage the beef?" Gunn asked.

"Jace got it from the railroad people. They're tryin' to get a spur line building."

"And what about the Sioux? Or hasn't anyone thought about them?"

"By the time the spur's built, there won't be any Sioux. Not around here, anyway."

"What makes you so sure of that, Selma? The nearest fort is Randall, and they haven't got a third of what they'd need to run the Hunkpatila out of the country, or onto a reservation."

Selma smiled. "They will have. Jace just got back from Randall. The commander there's been promoted to colonel and he's got more men comin' in. Anyway, they're fixin' to sit down and pow wow with the chiefs. Seth Kinkaid's settin' it all up."

Gunn's eyebrows raised in surprise. "What chiefs? When? Where?"

"Whoa, now," Selma said, holding out both hands. "One thing at a time. I don't know what chiefs. Jace said somethin' about one named Sinty, Sinta—somethin' like that."

"Sinte Galeshka?"

"Yeah, that was it. Anyway, the colonel over there at Randall wants to palaver with 'em. Jace figured to get in on it. He offered the tradin' post as the spot to do it."

"When is this supposed to take place?"

"Soon as they can talk to this here Sinty fella." She grinned. "The way I hear it if the talk don't go the way they want, the Army's just gonna arrest the chiefs an' the rest of 'em that show up. Without the chiefs, the Sioux'll head west or crawl to the reservation."

"Somebody's feeding you pap," Gunn said. "Seth Kinkaid would never be a party to a stunt like that. And I don't think Waddington would put his name to it, either."

"Maybe you're right, but it don't matter 'cause Colonel Waddington and ol' Kinkaid won't know nothin' about it. Jace heard that the railroad folks have put on a little pressure back east. Some gen'rul's gonna have plenty o' troops moved in between here and wherever them Sioux is camped. If the palaver is all right, they'll move right in. If not, they'll wait 'til Waddington and Kinkaid head back to Randall, then they'll move. Either way, the Indians lose."

"Son of a bitch," Gunn grumbled. The Sioux were planning an attack on Randall, Seth Kinkaid was setting up a council he believed to be sincere, Colonel Waddington wanted to talk before he acted and Washington had a double-cross in mind. The one man who knew it all was Gunn. Now the question was who did he tell what . . . first?

The bat-wings flew open and Selma and Gunn

looked up at the same time. Two men entered. The first wore two guns, strapped low, butts reversed in their holsters. Warm as it was, the second wore a poncho. Gunn caught a glimpse of the shotgun's barrel beneath it.

"The Lassiters," Selma said. She got up, took a deep breath and walked over to the bar. "Hiya boys. Come on in. First drink's on Selma Lee, after that, ever'thing gets expensive." She laughed.

The first man barely looked at her. His eyes had scanned the place, then fixed on Gunn. Since then, they'd never left him. The second man swatted Selma on the fanny, then pulled her close and nibbled on her ear.

"You just got about a quarter's worth, free," Selma said. Anything more, you pay for."

"Will, we're here on business," Clay Lassiter said, still staring at Gunn. " 'Til we get that done, you keep clear of women."

"Aw, Clay, you're tighter'n a hangman's noose." He reached for Selma and Selma dodged adroitly, laughing seductively.

"I told you, it'll cost you," she said.

"Get the hell away from 'im, woman!" Clay said. "You understand?"

"Yeah, Clay, sure, sure, I understand. Why don't you have a drink?"

"Coffee. Black and strong. Get it and bring it to the front table," Clay said.

"All right," Selma agreed.

Gunn had never met the Lassiters but he did know

them by reputation. He knew that Clay was wanted in half a dozen towns between St. Louis and Denver, and most men Gunn knew considered Will Lassiter half-crazy, as well as half-blind.

Gunn waited until the brothers had downed their first cups of coffee and Selma refilled them. When he got up, he noted Clay Lassiter tense and shift his position. Gunn walked straight to them.

"I'm your business," he said.

"You look law to me." Clay Lassiter eased his chair backwards. Gunn folded his arms across his chest.

"I'm not law. I'm here talking for Sinte Galeshka. About a mile out there's a Sioux named Crow King. He's got a poke for you."

"You think I'm stupid, mister? You think me'n my brother'd ride out o' here with you and straight into an ambush?"

"Nope. We ride just outside the post and you wait. I'll bring the Sioux down, out in the open, where you can see us and we can see the wagon."

"Wagon? What wagon you talkin' about?"

"The one you'll fetch while I get the Indian. We'll make the exchange right there and then we can both be on our way."

"Who are you, mister? How come you're dealin' for the Sioux?"

"I'm a blood brother. They trust me." Gunn paused for just a split second, shifting his own position slightly. "My name is Gunn."

Clay Lassiter was on his feet in a flash. Will brought his sawed-off around so that it was leveled at Gunn's groin. Gunn carefully pointed to his vest pocket. "You mind?" he asked.

"Not me," Clay said. "But if you move wrong, you will."

Gunn pulled out a pinch of gold dust, then another, and finally a third. He piled it on the table right under Will Lassiter's nose. Will's eyes got big. He grinned and his left hand came up to touch it. Gunn's boot shot out and hooked on the rung of Will's chair. Gunn pulled and Will went over backwards. His right hand snatched his Colt free of the holster, leveled it at Clay, while his left hand caught the barrel of the sawed-off shotgun, pulling it free of Will's faltering grip. Gunn stepped back.

"I don't like threats and I like it even less when a man points a shotgun at me," he said. "On top of that, I gave my word we'd do our business outside the post, and I intend to keep my word. Now, you two ride west to where I said. Get your wagon and I'll be there with the Indian and the rest of that." Gunn pointed to the gold dust with the barrel of the sawed-off.

"What about my shotgun, mister?"

"You'll get that back after we've done our business."

Gunn followed them outside Selma's place, then watched them ride out of sight. Selma stood beside him.

"You've brought yourself a passel of trouble, Gunn. Nobody tells Clay Lassiter what to do, most particular after pullin' down on 'im like that. He'll kill you, if not today, then tomorrow or next week. He won't forget."

"She's right," Jace Barker said, coming out of his

office next door. "I don't want you riding back in here, mister, not now, not ever Leastwise, not as long as Clay Lassiter and his brother're still breathin'."

"I'll keep it in mind, Barker," Gunn said. "But if the Lassiters want to try me, I'd just as soon get it over with. I don't like havin' to look over my shoulder." Gunn turned to Selma. "I want you to do me a favor."

"What's that?"

"Close up for a spell. Go back east. Omaha maybe, or St. Joe. There's going to be trouble out here." Gunn looked straight at Jace Barker. "A lot more big trouble than Clay Lassiter or Barker's Trading Post can handle. If you stay, you'll be right in the middle of it."

"You givin' the orders around here now, mister?" Jace asked.

"I'm not ordering, just suggesting," Gunn said. "If you do stay, you'll think back on this little conversation and know just how good a suggestion it was." Gunn walked off in the direction of the livery.

"What the hell was that all about?" Jace asked.

"I don't know for sure," Selma replied. "But I know Gunn and he doesn't say things like that unless he means it. I think I'll just follow his advice."

Crow King rode slightly behind Gunn as they approached the Lassiters. Gunn saw the look of hatred on Clay's face. He knew that if Clay Lassiter could do it, he would kill both of them, take the gold and the rifles. The two riders reined up. Gunn dismounted but Crow King didn't.

"You've seen some dust," Gunn said. He held up the poke and tossed it onto the wagon seat. "You can look at the rest after I've seen the rifles."

"Yeah, sure. Here," Clay said. "Try this one, or this one." He held two Winchesters out to Gunn. Gunn ignored both the words and the rifles. Instead he walked to the wagon, threw back the canvas and lifted an opened crate to the side. He glanced back at Clay.

"You mind?"

"Seems to me like you're callin' me a liar and a cheat," Clay said.

Gunn moved another crate, then yanked the bottom one to the ground. The old wood split wide open and several rifles fell out.

"Mind if I try one of these?" Clay Lassiter's eyes shifted quickly to Crow King. His eyes shifted to his brother, then back to Gunn. He smiled and shrugged.

"Why not, Gunn? I'd be a damn fool to cheat the Sioux, wouldn't I?"

Gunn didn't bother to answer. He picked up a rifle, a .44 like his own. He pulled a bullet from his vest pocket and loaded the weapon. He scanned the area around the wagon and his eyes fell on an empty whiskey bottle. He sighted and fired. The dirt flew up about two feet away. Gunn looked at Clay Lassiter.

"They ain't new," Clay said. "Didn't claim they was. That shot woulda killed an antelope or a deer."

"Antelope and deer don't shoot back." Gunn picked up another, loaded it and tossed it to Clay. "You try this one — real careful."

Clay Lassiter sighted on the same bottle and

squeezed off the round. The bottle shattered. Clay grinned broadly.

"Well, now, maybe it's the man holdin' the rifle makes it shoot wrong," he said. He tossed it back, hard. "I think all the testin's been done that needs to be done."

It was a tough point to argue. Gunn nodded. Clay walked to the wagon, opened the poke, then removed an empty sack from his hip pocket. He poured the gold dust from one to the other, slowly, eyeing it for signs of sand. He finished.

"Looks as good as them rifles," he said. "Seems to me our business is done."

"Not quite," Gunn said. He stepped away from the wagon spreading his legs for just the right balance. His right arm hung loose, almost like his shirt sleeve was empty. He noticed a slight frown wrinkling Clay Lassiter's brow. "I was told you'd be resentful of what happened back in Selma's place. Told me you don't forget. If that's right, let's settle it now."

"You callin' me out, Gunn?"

"Nope. Just asking if you want to call me."

Gunn had been there before. He could sense Clay Lassiter's feelings and he knew full well that Clay would like nothing better than to test himself against Gunn but, for the moment at least, Clay had lost the edge. It was that razor-thin advantage that every man has to have and at this moment, Gunn owned it.

Clay shrugged and smiled. "I was just bein' careful, Gunn, that's all. Wasn't you?"

"Yeah, Lassiter, I was." Gunn said. He relaxed, then

added, "I always am." Gunn threw the rifles back onto the wagon, then walked over to Crow King. "Ride the wagon back to where you were. I'll bring your mount and meet you in about an hour."

"If you don't return, Shadow Hand, the woman will still belong to Crippled Antelope."

"I'll return," Gunn said.

The big Sioux smiled and nodded. A few minutes later he was nearly out of sight.

The Lassiters had ridden to the south and Gunn knew he had to make one final trip to Barker's post.

## Chapter Seventeen

Seth Kinkaid bit another chunk of tobacco from his plug. He tucked the rest back into his pocket, then folded his arms. He had heard the Sioux approaching. In fact he got wind of them some five minutes earlier. Finally, three of them rode into view, approaching slowly. With an air of nonchalance, he raised one arm.

The Sioux made no sign of greeting, but rode directly to him. He was sitting against a huge willow tree.

"What is it you wish to speak about, Great Bear?" It was Sinte Galeshka who spoke.

"Army wants to palaver with you, Sinte Galeshka. You 'n' Kicking Bear. Colonel Waddington wants to meet you at Barker's place."

"The Blue Coats talked to Red Cloud, but there is no peace. They promised no wagons would come to the Rosebud, but they come. Why should we talk more?"

Seth shoved his hat back on his head and squinted. "You got me," he said. "I'm just totin' the message, that's all. Don't matter none to me whether you talk or not."

"You have always been a man who spoke the truth,"

Sinte Galeshka said. "Still, you fight against us. Why is this?"

"Simple enough, I'm white, you're Injun, 'n' when it comes to the nut cuttin' I gotta line up with my own."

"What do you think we should do?"

"I'm not much of a figurin' man, Sinte Galeshka. Got me no book learnin' a'tall, can just barely write my own name. But if'n I was to figure, I'd think about this. They's a heap more white people than they is Injuns. Now, talkin' ain't gonna stop all the killin', but it might save some of you. If you don't do nothin' but fight, there won't be no Sioux left."

"Do you believe the Blue Coat who sent you?"

Seth spit out his quid. "Yep. But that don't mean nothin'. Colonel Waddington's just a little man. The folks back in Washin'ton can change anything they want. I told Waddington 'n' I'm tellin' you. I don't make no promise I can't keep, personal."

"When is the talk to be?"

"Soon. Two, maybe three days."

"If we talk but cannot hear each other, what will happen?"

"I reckon the Army'll come after you, Sinte Galeshka. They'll drive you from your village, round you up and put you on a reservation."

"We will fight."

"I figure you will," Seth said. "But you won't win. Talk's cheap, Sinte Galeshka, but at least it buys time."

"Great Bear, if you were in my place, what would you do?"

"Same as you're doin'. I'd fight."

"And would you win?"

"Nope." Seth offered Sinte Galeshka a chew from his

tobacco. The Indian took a bite, then handed it back. Seth took a chew, poked a few loose strands into his mouth, then worked it to one side so he could speak. "I seen your wife and babies. I got neither. If'n I did, maybe I'd talk more 'n' fight less." Seth saw that Sinte Galeshka was beginning to get a little green, so he spit out his quid to signal to the Indian that he could do the same thing.

Sinte Galeshka spat, then wiped his chin.

"Go to the fort, Great Bear. Tell the Blue Coat chief I will do this thing. I cannot speak for Kicking Bear, but if he says this is good, we will come together to the white man's trading post. We will do this in four days."

"I'll tell 'em."

"Will you sit with the soldiers, Great Bear?"

"Nope," Seth said. "If I sat with them, I'd be givin' my word that what they say is true. Like I told you, Sinte Galeshka, if I can't keep it personal, I don't make no promises. I just hope I don't have to come chasin' after you."

"The day we meet will be a good day to die," Sinte Galeshka said.

"That's sort of the way I figure it."

The Indians started to leave, then Sinte Galeshka turned toward Seth. "Are you friend to the one we call Shadow Hand?"

"Are you talking about Gunn?"

"Yes. That is what the Christian men call him."

"I was. I hear the Crow got 'im."

"It is not so. He killed the white buffalo and is now the blood brother to Sinte Galeshka. I will speak to him of this thing."

"How long's he been with you?"

"Many days now. Soon, he will ride free."

"I'll be damned." Seth scratched his head and laughed. "I just couldn't figure no Crow knockin' off Gunn. Well, now, Sinte Galeshka, you tell ole Gunn to keep his hair. He owes me a jug."

"I do not understand this thing."

"Never mind. Just tell 'im to get on back to Fort Randall where he belongs."


Selma Lee answered the knock at her door and the drop of her jaw revealed her surprise at seeing Gunn.

"You don't listen real good, do you?" Then she tilted her head in a gesture of query. "Or is Clay Lassiter dead?"

"Not as I know of."

"If Jace saw you, he'd be mad as hell."

"He didn't, but it makes no difference." He handed Selma an envelope. It was thick, sealed and bore the name Josiah Waddington.

"Colonel Waddington? Why give it to me?"

"Take it to him when you go east. Make sure he gets it. He may even show up before you leave."

"What the hell makes you think I'm going to leave?"

"Because you know damned well I wouldn't ask you to if I didn't have a good reason."

"When will I see you again, Gunn?"

"There's lots of trails out there, Selma," Gunn said. "And they all cross at one time or another." He leaned down and kissed her, gently.

Jace Barker was waiting just outside. Gunn barely glanced at him as he walked to Esquire.

"I told you not to ride back here, Gunn, and I meant

it." Gunn ignored him and mounted his horse. He backed Esquire about three steps, then turned east. "Did you hear me, you son of a bitch?" Gunn rode by him without a word. "Face me, Gunn! Face me right now!" Gunn spurred his horse and Esquire broke into a trot. "I'll cut you down from here!" Gunn didn't even look back.

Selma stepped outside, took in the scenario, then laughed.

"It's your lucky day, Jace. You ought to play some poker."

"What the hell are you talkin' about?" he shouted.

"You might've made him mad. Then he woulda faced you."

"You think I'm through with him?"

"Nope," Selma said. "But I always figured you were none too bright anyway."


Gunn didn't like the feel of things, even before he got to the stand of trees where he was to meet Crow King. It was too quiet and he was back well ahead of the hour he'd said. The big Sioux should be stirring around to see who was riding in.

"Crow King?" he called. There was no reply. Gunn dismounted and patted Esquire's neck as he dropped the reins. "Stay put," he said. He looked at the ground and could see the deep ruts of the wagon wheels in the mud. He followed them, and went only another three hundred yards or so before he saw the wagon. It was overturned and he could see long crates broken open. He ran to it.

The scene revealed everything Gunn needed to

know. There were no rifles still in crates. They were scattered about, some with broken stocks, others half in the water where they had been thrown. There were many more crates than there were rifles. The other crates had been filled with rocks.

"Son of a bitch!" Gunn said aloud. He hadn't checked the crates on the opposite side of the wagon. He'd been taken in like a greenhorn. The Sioux had paid for a wagonload of Winchesters and gotten maybe two dozen. Unshod pony tracks headed off to the south.

"Crow King, you crazy bastard, the Lassiters will cut your liver out."

Gunn found one intact rifle and half a box of ammunition. He grabbed several handfuls of shells, mounted up and rode hard, along the trail Crow King had taken.

The sun was high and hot. Half a dozen buzzards circled at different heights over a spot along the river. Gunn got a knot in his stomach and rode on.

Crow King was still alive, though just barely. He was propped against a tree and Gunn could see the trail of blood that revealed the path of Crow King's agonizing crawl. The Indian had been shot in the stomach with a load of double-aught shot. He had both hands over the hole, trying to hold his insides in, while blood still spilled through his fingers. His eyes were fluttering.

"Crow King!" Gunn knelt beside his Indian friend. "You crazy son of a bitch, why didn't you wait for me like I said?"

"We were cheated, Shadow Hand."

"Yeah, I saw. But we could have gone after them together."

"The one with the eye that cannot see now has an arm that cannot work," Crow King said. "I cut him with my knife before he shot me."

"Which way did they go?"

Crow King coughed and blood spewed from his mouth. "I heard them say they would go to—" he coughed again and gagged. Gunn knew there was no point in telling Crow King to remain quiet. The big Sioux was finished, and Gunn needed the information.

"Where, Crow King? Where were they going?"

"The place called Willow Bend."

Crow King was silent for a few moments, then he asked for water. Gunn knew that you shouldn't give water to people with belly wounds, but he knew also that was primarily for people who might have a chance to survive. Crow King had no chance and if water would help ease his suffering, then water he would have. Crow King took several deep gulps, drinking as a man who had been for days on the desert. Gunn watched as some of the water spilled out of the wound in his stomach, along with more blood. Crow King finally slaked his thirst, then leaned his head back against the tree. He breathed hard for a couple of minutes more, then stopped.

Gunn buried him in a shallow grave, just to keep the critters away. He would come back later and move Crow King's body back to the village where he would be given a warrior's burial.

Willow Bend had been a way station and a rest stop

for men scouting for the Army at one time. Now it was a haven for gunnies and transient thieves. An ex-Army doctor gone sour ran the place. He kept two or three women around to serve drinks or anything else they could charge for and he charged plenty. Gunn topped a hill overlooking it about midafternoon. He could see half a dozen horses tethered to the hitching rail, among them Clay and Will Lassiter's.

There were three buildings at Willow Bend, the main house, a two-room soddy, and a smaller frame building about twenty yards behind. It was here that the girls sometimes provided their services. The third was a smokehouse. Gunn worked his way into the latter and found what he was looking for: coal oil.

He saturated two rag-wrapped torches and dumped the rest around the base of the flimsy building. He struck a match to it and hurried outside. He made his way to the "girl's" place and burst through the front door. A man sat up on the edge of the bed, then started to reach for his handgun.

"Don't do it," Gunn said sharply. "I got no quarrel with you, I don't want to kill you. Lie back down, face down."

The man complied. The girl next to him instinctively pulled the covers high enough to hide her breasts. Gunn grinned.

The smokehouse burst into full flame. Two men came around the corner of the soddy, yelling. Neither of them was Clay Lassiter. Gunn was crouched at the glassless window. The bed creaked. Gunn whirled. The man on the bed was twisting to get into position. Gunn got to him in one step and brought the butt of the rifle down on the man's face, sending a couple of teeth flying as he knocked him cold. The girl screamed.

Gunn kicked the door open and stepped outside, the rifle firm against his shoulder. One of the men was wearing a gun, the other was unarmed.

"I got not quarrel with you two," Gunn called to them. "Why don't we keep it that way?"

"You set fire to my smokehouse, mister?"

"I did."

"Then we got a quarrel."

"Too bad," Gunn said. "I'm here for Clay and Will Lassiter."

The girl suddenly pushed hard on Gunn's back, hard enough to knock him off balance. He knew his only chance was to go ahead with what she'd started. He fell to the ground, then rolled.

The man with the gun cleared leather but his shot was too late to hit Gunn. The girl groaned and fell backwards. Gunn cut him down with the Winchester. The second man darted for the soddy but he was unarmed so Gunn let him go. He got to his feet.

Two more men, one who looked like a breed, stepped into view. At the opposite corner of the soddy a voice got Gunn's attention.

"You lookin' fer us, Gunn?"

"Not anymore," Gunn said.

Clay Lassiter stepped away from the building. He was grinning as he took a wide stance and dug his bootheels into the soft ground. Will stayed near the edge of the building. His right hand was in a sling, probably the work of the rogue doctor. Will wasn't carrying his shotgun.

"My brother Will got cut up good by that Injun friend of yours. I reckon he's gonna have to sit this one out. But you got me, 'n' Brill, 'n' Hank," Clay said, smiling broadly. "You figure you're good enough to take all of us?"

"Don't know," Gunn said. "So for now, I'll just concentrate on you."

Lassiter's grin faded to a twisted smile, then disappeared. "I heard you took three good men down at Fort Kearny. That true? Or did you backshoot two of 'em with a Winchester?"

It was an old ruse, talking down the man you're facing, rile him, get the edge. Gunn didn't respond. He was mentally gauging distances and the spread of his targets.

Gunn watched Lassiter's lips moving. He even caught a word or two, though he wasn't listening. "I don't think . . . try . . . that good." When the words stopped, Lassiter would make his move. Gunn would make his, just a split-second sooner.

Gunn ignored the words and his eyes never left Lassiter's face. He saw the lips stop, the hands move, the glint of the sun catching the blued steel barrel of Lassiter's pistol. Gunn's Colt cracked twice. The man called Brill fell straight back. His gun had not yet cleared its holster. The man called Hank got off a shot. It dug up the dirt twenty feet in front of Gunn. Hank was dead before he hit the ground.

Clay Lassiter was fast, damned fast, but he used a reverse-grip draw. It took time. Not much, but enough for Gunn to take out the others. Lassiter's shot put a bullet through the fleshy part of Gunn's left shoulder, just at the armpit. Gunn winced but took his time, that extra fraction of a second. The Colt's third bullet went straight into Clay Lassiter's heart, even as he got off a second shot. The second shot tore through Gunn's pant leg, creasing the flesh just below his hip.

"You rotten son of a bitch!"

Gunn had completely forgotten about Will. Will had somehow found the time to get mounted and his animal reared so that Gunn's line of fire was obscured. Will cradled the shotgun in his left arm, and as his horse came back down, the shotgun boomed.

Gunn heard the deadly pellets ripping into the wood of the shack behind him. Will Lassiter wheeled the horse back to his right but there was no time to fire again. Gunn's shot found the mark.

Two more men appeared at the corner of the soddy.

"Don't crowd it," Gunn said. The men saw the six bodies lying on the ground, so they heeded his words.

Gunn retrieved the gold dust, then rode out of the settlement without looking back. He didn't have to. No one wanted to tangle with him, no matter what their advantage might be.

"That bastard's got somethin' stuck in his craw," said one, his voice quivering. "Acts like he's in the funeral business."

"Just make damned sure it ain't your funeral he's plannin'," said the other man, swallowing hard.

"Yeah. For damned sure."

Gunn rode out of sight, but not out of mind.

## Chapter Eighteen

Gunn's arrival back at the village was hardly what he'd expected. He had treated his shoulder wound as best he could. The bullet had passed through harmlessly, but he was still pretty queasy. He was yanked from his horse, disarmed, stripped to the waist and covered with white paint, then tied to a pole in front of the council lodge.

Throughout the evening the Indians danced a funeral dance for Crow King, then, finally, fell silent. Two warriors freed Gunn and dragged him before Sinte Galeshka.

"Sinte Galeshka, why am I being treated like this?"

"You were sent for rifles, Shadow Hand. You bring no rifles. Where is Crow King?"

"Those men tried to cheat you, Sinte Galeshka. They killed Crow King. I avenged his death and I returned the gold."

"Crippled Antelope and the other young ones want to kill you."

"And you, Sinte Galeshka? What do you want?"

"My mind is not clear," Sinte Galeshka said. "You did not have to return, but you did. I must think more about this. We will not speak of it now. I go to the trading post to meet with the soldiers. When this is done, we shall speak again. Then I will know what to do."

"You don't have that long," Gunn said. "We need to talk now." He moved toward Sinte Galeshka, and never heard the noise behind him. Blackness enveloped him.

Gunn's return to consciousness was accompanied by a soft warmth and a scent he'd smelled before. It seemed many hands were caressing his aching body. In fact, there were four. His head hurt, but passion pushed pain aside. Deer Spirit and Bright Moon touched him everywhere, all over, and each touch brought a bright fever to his flesh. He moaned softly as Deer Spirit positioned herself atop him.

"Touch me there," Bright Moon said. She directed Gunn's hand to the velvety softness of her inner thigh and his fingers instinctively changed course to the recesses of her womanhood. His cock swelled to a bone hardness as his free hand found Bright Moon's breasts. He squeezed gently and his fingers kneaded the mounds and the hardened nipple of first one, then the other breast. She groaned and her body writhed with pleasure.

Deer Spirit's fingers dug into Gunn's flesh. Her lips parted, her eyes closed and the juices flowed. She let out a little whimper of delight as her body broke into a vibrating moment of climax. Then she pulled free, still stroking Gunn's aching rod with her hand. She moved aside and Bright Moon mounted him. Gunn tried to speak but she leaned forward and thrust a nipple into his mouth.

Bright Moon moved her knees forward so that Gunn could move his hips freely. He did so instinctively, his still-hardened member pounding deep within her moist flesh. He could feel his own climax welling up from within him and he moved his hands to Bright Moon's hips. He pushed, hard, and slipped his fingers down along her stomach until they reached her most sensitive core. The combination stiffened her body instantly. Gunn pumped faster and Bright Moon moaned her pleasure in an explosive ripple of delight. She, too, found fulfillment and a moment later she rolled free of him, leaving him unsatisfied.

The two Indian maidens got to their feet, quickly dressed, and slipped from Gunn's tipi.

"Son of a bitch," Gunn mumbled. The pain of frustration in his groin was severe. He could feel the wetness on his thighs and stomach. He chuckled. If ever the expression "rode hard and put away wet" fit, it fit now.

Gunn heard a noise, soft, like a whimper. He raised to his elbows.

"Is that a squaw's revenge?" It was the voice of Lisa Briggs.

"What the hell are you doing here?"

"I really didn't have any choice. I'm tied up." Her tone wasn't angry, it was too heavy, breathy for anger. He moved over to her and loosened the ropes.

"Did they hurt you?" he asked.

"No."

By now they could see each other clearly. Gunn noticed her eyes fixed to his still-stiff cock.

"I've never . . . I've never been with a man," she said.

She reached out slowly, hesitantly, touch his manhood. He felt her fingers against it, heard the sharp intake of breath.

"Lisa, maybe you'd better—" he started, but she cut him off.

"I—I can't help myself," she whispered. "I have the strangest desire to to . . . to . . ." Without another word she leaned over and took him in her mouth. She sucked, pulling gently, then licking, then sucking again. Finally she pulled away from him, then lay on her back, her thighs spread wide. She licked her lips, squeezed her own breasts, then held her arms out to him. "Please," she said. "I want you in me, please."

"Not quite yet," Gunn said. He moved to her, then down her lithe, young body until he reached the little mound at the junction of her legs. He let his tongue ply this new territory, until her breathing was coming in short, rapid gasps. Then he moved over her.

Gunn was conscious of being more gentle than usual, but she was a virgin and winced with a quick pain when he first entered her. That passed quickly.

"Oh, yes. Do it, do it to me. Fill me with it," she moaned.

Gunn had been primed. Bright Moon and Deer Spirit had done the job to perfection. Now he thrust deep and hard into her young womanhood. Their flesh molded into a single knot of sensation, their juices flowed together until there was no more stopping.

"Oooh, yes, yes, YES!" Lisa screamed, a muffled, passionate sound. Gunn groaned, too, as, at last, he reached the pinnacle of pleasure.

They lay side by side and said nothing for a long time.

"I've never done that before. I never dreamed I could enjoy it so much. I always thought I would feel . . . dirty—after I did it. Do you think that makes me a whore?"

Gunn smiled. "You're not a whore, Lisa."

"Who are you?" Lisa said. She smiled. "I would at least like to know the name of the man who took my innocence."

"Seems to me there was as much givin' as takin'," Gunn said.

Lisa laughed, a small, lilting laugh like the bubbling of a brook.

"I guess you're right," she said.

"My name is Gunn. I'm scouting for the Army."

"Gunn? You're Gunn?"

"Yeah." Now he raised up. Her tone implied more than a casual familiarity with his name.

"My uncle told me about you, about a gunfight in Cheyenne. Could that be you?"

"Could be."

"How did you? I mean, those Indian women, you walking around here in war paint like a savage—what's going on?"

"It's a long story and I'll tell it to you sometime. Let's just say that I'd rather not be here if I could help it."

"Are they going to kill us?"

"I don't think so," Gunn said. "But either way we've got to ride out. If we don't, there'll be a blood bath on the Rosebud."

"Would it help if you had my pistol?"

"What? You mean you still have it?"

"Yes. I dug a hole and hid it."

"Where?"

"In the other tipi, where I was before."

"Tomorrow, Lisa, we'll figure a way to get it and get out of here."

Tomorrow, he thought wryly. He didn't want to tell her, but . . .

There might not be any tomorrow.

For either of them.

## Chapter Nineteen

It wasn't easy for Sinte Galeshka to talk Kicking Bear into making the trip to Barker's post with him. He decided to go, only because they had been unsuccessful in getting repeating rifles and he knew that without them, taking Fort Randall would be next to impossible.

The two chiefs led a delegation of a dozen Sioux, medicine men from both tribes, as well as hunters and warriors. They decided to camp on the Rosebud, then move on the next day to keep a noon meeting with Colonel Waddington.

Even as the Indians left their village, the Fifth Cavalry regiment had already reached the Niobrara river. There, they split into two forces which would converge on the Hunkpatila village from both east and west when a rider from the trading post reached them. The outcome of the council made no difference. Peacefully or otherwise, the Hunkpatila would be moved.

Gunn and Lisa Briggs were well guarded, but Gunn raised enough of a ruckus to finally get Crippled Antelope to his tipi.

"I want to see Sinte Galeshka," Gunn said.

"He rode out with the rising of the sun. Tomorrow he will meet with the Blue Coat chief and hear more lies. But the lies will not stop me from leading our warriors against the fort."

Gunn had nothing to lose, so he took a deep breath.

"Damn it, Crippled Antelope, you've already been lied to. The Army is laying a trap for you. Not even Colonel Waddington knows. Ride to Sinte Galeshka and tell him."

"What trick do you play, Shadow Hand?"

"None. I heard of this trap from someone at the trading post."

The Sioux smiled cynically. "You return with Crow King dead and without guns to tell me of a trap. But you said nothing to Sinte Galeshka to stop him from going. I think you said nothing because he can see into your heart to tell if you are lying. Well, I can tell if you are lying too."

"I'm not lying, Crippled Antelope. Take some warriors, ride west and south. You'll find soldiers, hundreds of them, moving this way."

Crippled Antelope eyed Gunn and Lisa, then he turned in disgust and started out.

Gunn looked at Lisa and shook his head. Finally he took a deep breath. "Wait," he called. Crippled Antelope turned back. "Go and look for the soldiers. Take her to your tipi, where you kept her before. If you don't find the soldiers, she will be your woman. I will give her to you."

"I can take her now, Shadow Hand."

"Yeah, you can, but you won't. I'm a blood brother

and you would have to answer to Sinte Galeshka. If I give her to you, you won't have to answer to anyone. If I am lying, she is yours."

Crippled Antelope wanted Lisa, as much to repay Gunn for taking Bright Moon as anything else. Gunn knew this and was counting on it. Finally the Sioux grabbed Lisa's arm and pulled her with him. Gunn watched as he tossed her back into the tipi where she'd hidden the pistol. So far, so good, he thought.

Seth Kinkaid had ridden back to a prearranged rendezvous with Sergeant-Major Mayhew after his meeting with Sinte Galeshka. Mayhew had tried to get Seth to sit in on the council but the old scout would have no part of it. Once he delivered the message, he rode back west, headed for Fort Robinson. The night Gunn had returned to the Hunkpatila village, Seth camped along the Niobrara. He broke camp before daylight and was making his trip a leisurely one.

Seth had just watered his horse and pack mule when he looked up and saw a cloud of dust to the north. What was it he saw? A buffalo herd? Surely not, not one this big, this far south, this time of the year. He mounted and rode toward the dust. Finally he reached a ridge from where he could see for miles. What he saw shocked even him. Half an hour later, he reached the head of the regiment.

"You're mister Kinkaid, I believe."

Seth looked at the shoulder boards of the soldier who spoke to him. He was a major general. Seth's eyes followed the long, blue column, then returned to the officer.

"I be Kinkaid. Where you bound for, Gen'rul?"

"We're campaigning against the hostiles along the Rosebud. We're the Fifth Cavalry out of Forts Laramie and Sedgewick."

Seth removed his hat and scratched his head, then twisted in his saddle and looked back from the way he had come. "That's mighty strange," he said.

"What's strange about it?"

"Gen'rul, they ain't no hostiles along the Rosebud. Leastwise, not yet they ain't. They's only Hunkpatila and you may not know it, but they'll be meetin' tomorrow with Colonel Waddington out o' Fort Randall."

"I'm not at liberty to discuss the matter with you, sir," the general said. Then he smiled and added, "But let me assure you that I am quite aware of the talks. Be that as it may, the outcome of those talks will make little difference to me."

Seth Kinkaid didn't need a picture painted for him. He was as mad as the big bear he resembled. He had been used.

"Well, sir," Seth said calmly. "Good luck to you then." He gave a nonchalant wave and rode along the column a short distance before he turned back south. Once he was out of sight of the column, Seth dismounted. He removed the gear from his pack horse, stowed it under some nearby trees and slapped the animal's flanks. A few minutes later he remounted and spurred his horse to a full gallop, headed east.

Nearly three hours had passed since Gunn made his deal with Crippled Antelope. He was beginning to have doubts about it. No one had ridden from the village. Gunn rolled his last smoke before he discovered that he had no match. He stuck his head outside where there were two warriors standing guard. He held out his cigarette.

"Fire," he said.

There was a small cooking fire burning nearby and one of the warriors nodded. Gunn walked to the blaze and crouched down. As he reached for a flaming brand, Crippled Antelope and half a dozen warriors galloped through the village. Gunn watched them pass, then lit his cigarette, taking the time to eye the other tipis. He finally spotted the one where Lisa Briggs was being held.

"Go now," one of the warriors said, grabbing his arm. Gunn looked at him and nodded. He'd have to come up with some idea to get to Lisa, and he had to do it before Crippled Antelope returned.

Back in the tipi, Gunn tried to relax, to free his thoughts and concentrate on a plan. He found it difficult. His mind kept running to the Indian plan to take Fort Randall, and the U.S. Government's doublecross. It really made no difference which one happened first, the end result would be the same either way. Certainly if the combined Indian forces attained their goal, other tribes would be easily drawn into an alliance. If the government trap was sprung first, the remaining free tribes would form an alliance. Gunn caught the glimpse of a shadow and looked up.

"I have brought food for you, Shadow Hand."

"Thanks," he said. "Did someone take food to the white girl?"

"I did." Bright Moon handed Gunn a small, woven basket. He saw some dried buffalo meat, a piece of hard bread.

Bright Moon glanced over her shoulder, then moved closer to Gunn. "Crippled Antelope will take the white woman from you, Shadow Hand. His spirit is sick. He will not listen to Sinte Galeshka or any of the chiefs."

"Why, Bright Moon? Won't Crippled Antelope himself be a chief some day?"

"It would have been so, but a bad thing has happened," Bright Moon said. "One day when Crippled Antelope was but a boy, he had a vision. In his vision he was by a tree and the earth shook beneath his feet and the sacred white buffalo charged him. Crippled Antelope killed the sacred buffalo and wore the horns on his head and became the greatest Sioux chief."

"And what went wrong?"

"Crippled Antelope went before the Shaman and asked for guidance. The Shaman told him his vision was not of a white buffalo, but of a white man who only looked like a buffalo, and that only a spirit would die."

"Whose spirit, Bright Moon?"

"Crippled Antelope's." Bright Moon backed from the tipi, pointing, one last time, to the basket of food.

When Bright Moon was gone, Gunn reached down into the basket for a piece of bread. His hand fell on something hard, and when he moved the bread to one side, he saw Lisa's little pistol.

Seth Kinkaid got his second surprise of the day when he reached the confluence of the Niobrara and Rosebud rivers. A line of Sioux, Crow and Cheyenne was strung south beyond his vision. They were moving northwest. Seth had no trouble riding through to the chiefs. One of them was his old friend, Red Cloud.

"Do you ride for the Blue Coats, Great Bear?"

"I was," Seth admitted. "But I ain't no more. What brings you north, Red Cloud?"

"I cannot say."

"You're ridin' into a trap, my friend. Army's got a whole regiment waitin' for you." Seth pointed west. "Over there on the Niobrar'."

Red Cloud frowned.

"Why do you tell us?"

" 'Cause I set up a parley between Sinte Galeshka and Colonel Waddington. I never lied to the Sioux before 'n' I didn't know I was lyin' this time. I don't want to be no party to it."

"We ride only to the Paha Sapa," Red Cloud said.

Seth didn't buy it. "With Crow and Cheyenne? Ain't none o' my affair, Red Cloud, but they's somethin' wrong here."

"We wish no fight with the pony soldiers," Red Cloud said.

"Maybe not," Seth said. "But you're gonna have one if'n they see all this. Best thing you kin do is hightail it on back down to the Platte. I'll ride on and talk to Sinte Galeshka and after, I'll get word to you."

Red Cloud was skeptical and there were other chiefs with him he'd have to talk to about all this. He conferred with the others quietly, while Seth chewed on his tobacco and waited patiently. Finally the old chief came back to him.

"We will make camp here. You ride to Sinte Galeshka. When you return we will know what to do."

Seth didn't like it much. He was caught sure. Square between a rock and a mighty hard place.

# Chapter Twenty

Gunn made his move. He let out a howl, just loud enough for his two guards to hear. He was counting on the contrast between the bright sunshine outside and the nearly total darkness in the tipi to give him the edge he needed.

It worked. He knocked both Indians out, bound and gagged them, then walked, almost casually, over to Lisa Briggs' tipi. He stepped in, placing his index finger across his lips as he did so. He knelt beside her.

"I'm going to try to find my clothes and weapons," Gunn said.

"They're in Crippled Antelope's tipi," Lisa said. She moved to the door flap and pointed. "That one."

Gunn looked and saw that there was no one around.

"The Indian girl is in there, the one I gave the pistol to," Lisa said.

"Bright Moon? How'd you know to trust her?"

"She undressed me the first day and saw the gun. She told me to bury it."

"I'll be damned," Gunn said.

Gunn was certain no one paid any attention to him when he walked to Crippled Antelope's tipi and slipped in. Bright Moon sat in its center, staring down at a pile of buffalo bones. She looked up.

"I've got no time," he said, "except to say thank you. Do you understand that?"

Bright Moon nodded and pointed to a hide. Gunn lifted it and saw his clothes, his Colt and Winchester. He dressed quickly.

Bright Moon stood before him. "The Great Spirit has spoken to me. What he says is there." She pointed to the bones. "I will not be the woman of Crippled Antelope."

"Bright Moon, I want to help you but . . ."

Bright Moon shook her head. "I do not mean I will be your woman. I will be no man's woman. Tatanka Wakan has called me."

"No, you'll be fine. And I'll be back, I promise you that."

"Your horse, Shadow Hand. I took him to the big tree by the river. There is also one for the white girl."

"Thanks again," Gunn said. He hurried back to Lisa and when he was certain they were clear, they left her tipi and hurried to the river. Indeed, Esquire was saddled and waiting as was a stolen cavalry mount. Gunn knew there was no time to waste. As soon as his former guards were discovered, the Hunkpatila would send warriors after them. He also knew that if Bright Moon's assistance was discovered, she would indeed join the Great Spirit.

Gunn knew just about where Sinte Galeshka would be camped. It was there that Lisa thought they were going. Instead, Gunn headed them north after they cleared the village.

"I thought you wanted to ride to Fort Randall."

147

"We're going to the trading post," Gunn said. "That's where we'll find Colonel Waddington." Gunn knew he'd have no time to argue with Sinte Galeshka. He hoped that, somehow, Selma Lee had managed to get his message to Waddington.

Selma Lee hadn't found an opportunity to get to Colonel Waddington yet and any such chance was about to be eliminated.

"You may as well go on and pour yourself a drink," Jason Barker told her. "You sure as hell ain't goin nowhere."

"The hell I'm not. Like I told you before, Gunn don't lie."

"After this here powwow is over with, Selma Lee, I don't give a shit what you do. Till then, you're stayin right here."

Selma Lee stepped forward to slap his face but Jace was too fast for her. He grabbed her arms and hurled her backwards. She fell against her carpetbag and i was thrown clear of the envelope she had put under it Jace's eyes caught the name. He moved to it, back handed Selma Lee as she tried to grab it, then ripped i open.

"Give that to me," she demanded.

"You bitch!" He slapped her once, then again. Bloo spewed from her nose. "I ought to kill you." She pushed back from him, cowering now in the corner of th room. "I shoulda killed Gunn."

"I wish to hell you would've tried," Selma Lee said

"You leave this room and I will kill you," Jason said He slammed the door behind him and Selma Le heard the key turn in the lock.

Jace went directly to the saloon. His younger brother had just returned from Fort Pierre.

"I want you to keep an eye on Selma Lee, Brad. She's not to be leavin' her room," Jace said.

"How come?"

"Don't argue with me, boy, just do what I tell you. I'm ridin' out to the Army's camp to talk to the colonel."

"Yeah, sure, Jace. Whatever you say."

Colonel Waddington and the others who would sit in council with the Sioux were camped about half an hour's ride from Barker's post. By arrangement, both whites and Indians were to ride in at the same time. Jace found Waddington busying himself with the treaty proposals.

"Mister Barker?" Colonel Wadddington said, clearly surprised to see Jace. "Is there a problem?"

"Don't think so, Colonel," Jace said, his voice calm. He dismounted. "But I'd like to take some precautions just the same."

"Precautions? What kind of precautions?"

"There's been some talk, Colonel. You know the kind, white settlers who don't believe in any treaties, malcontents with more to gain if you're fightin' Sioux than talkin' with 'em. We don't need any of 'em ridin' in tomorrow and stirrin' up trouble."

"I agree, sir. I'll post sentires accordingly."

Jace looked down, shuffling his feet.

"Something else?"

"Well, sir, I don't claim to know much 'bout these kinds of things, Colonel. But it just seems to me that a bunch of armed soldiers standin' guard might scare the Sioux."

Waddington thought about it for a moment, then nodded his head. "Yes, I suppose that's true," he said.

"On the other hand," Jace went on, "I got me half a dozen men workin' for me that can prob'ly handle it. Why don't you let me keep 'em out? That is if anybody does try to ride in. Injuns won't pay no mind to my men."

"That seems reasonable, sir. Yes, quite reasonable. Very well, Mister Barker, see to it and the Army will be grateful for your loyalty and assistance."

"Whatever you say, Colonel," Jace said. "I'll see to it and there'll be no trouble, you can be sure of that."

## Chapter Twenty-one

It was nearing dusk by the time Gunn and Lisa reached the top of the ridge overlooking Barker's post. Gunn spotted the smoke in the distance and pointed.

"Indians?" Lisa asked.

"Not likely. It's probably Colonel Waddington. Either way, it looks like we made it in plenty of time."

"Are we riding into the trading post?"

"Nope, straight to the camp." They followed the ridge east until it sloped down to the river. When they reached the ford, they found themselves facing two men with rifles.

"Well, now," one of the men said. "Jace is gonna be real pleased to see you again." He eyed Lisa, covering every curve on her body. He grinned. "You got real nice trail company."

"What I've got," Gunn retorted, "is business with the Army. That their camp down river?"

"It's Army, but you ain't ridin' to it. Nobody is 'til Jace says so." The man raised his rifle higher and motioned with the barrel. "Let's go to the post."

The other man stepped forward. "You won't be needin' that Colt, Mister Gunn. Why don't you just unbuckle it? Then the rifle."

Gunn reached easy with his left hand to Lisa's little pistol. He had tucked it into his waistband before leaving the village, and now his vest covered the butt. The two gunnies were looking at the Colt and didn't realize until too late that he had drawn on them. Both men drew. Neither man got off a shot. He snorted, blowing out the acrid smoke that clogged his nostrils.

"Get to the Army," Gunn shouted at Lisa. "Get to Colonel Waddington. Tell him everything you know. I'll be there as soon as I can." Even as he spoke, he slapped the flank of Lisa's horse and it broke into a run. Gunn knew the shots would be heard by someone else. He headed toward the trading post.

Gunn rode up behind the livery barn. There he dismounted, tethered Esquire to a loose board and pulled the Winchester. He walked around the building. He was not in a good spot. What light remained was facing him and it made for long, low shadows.

Gunn eyed the street, saw no movement and trotted to the side opposite the livery. He started toward the saloon, hugging the buildings. A rifle shot cracked and wood splintered just above Gunn's head. He dropped to one knee, firing the Winchester almost at the same time. A man grabbed at his chest, staggered on the rooftop opposite Gunn's position, then fell forward. His body made a sickening thud as it struck a horse trough.

"You're finished, Gunn!"

Gunn whirled, his hands operating the lever action

and trigger of the rifle like they were part of it. He fired three rapid shots. He'd guessed right. Two more were dead.

The street was silent again. He had only two rounds left in the rifle. He started up the street, this time walking down its middle. Halfway to the saloon, two men emerged and took up spots in the street. One of them was Jason Barker.

"You won't yellow belly on me this time, Gunn," Barker called. Gunn kept walking. He stopped when he'd covered about half the distance to where the men stood. Carefully, Gunn lowered the Winchester.

"No, Barker, I won't," he said.

"Gunn, behind you!" It was Selma Lee. Gunn dropped, rolled, twisted and fired. The man never cleared leather. Gunn's momentum carried him another full turn, away from a whining bullet which kicked up dirt inches away. At that moment he heard the deep, deadly boom of a .50-caliber Sharps. He saw Jason Barker's body tossed toward him like a rag doll. The man beside Jason fired, his bullet singing over Gunn's head. Gunn squeezed off a round and saw the man's left kneecap turn to red jelly. He went down, moaning, holding his knee.

As Gunn got up, brushing himself off, he saw the silhouette of a huge man step from the shadows.

"Seems to me like that there'd be two jugs you owe me now, Gunn."

"You callin' in my marker, Seth?"

"Yep. If'n I don't, you're likely to get yourself kilt before I can collect."

"I'm not sure we're finished."

"We're finished. They was another one back up the street there but I took care of him."

"I didn't hear the Sharps."

"Didn't want to distract your shootin'," Seth said. He reached behind him and hauled out his knife. "Took him out with my Arkansas toothpick."

Colonel Waddington's face went from a paled shock to red with anger. He rode at the head of a twelve-man patrol as soon as Lisa talked to him, and met Gunn and Seth Kinkaid at Abe's, where he heard the rest of the story.

"You've stopped the bloodiest confrontation yet, gentlemen," he told them.

"I'm afraid we haven't, Colonel," Gunn replied. "There's still Sinte Galeshka and Kicking Bear to talk to—and convince. And Red Cloud is already geared for an attack. Seth will have to convince him and the others to ride back south."

"And," Seth added. "They's that gen'rul and the Fifth. He didn't seem too interested in doin' anythin' but fightin'."

"I'll get back to Randall and telegraph St. Louis. Whoever he is, we'll put a stop to it."

"There's no time for that, Colonel," Gunn said. "All this business with the railroad and Washington—well, you should be the one to handle it, but that regiment of cavalry has to be stopped right away."

"He wouldn't defy a direct order from Washington," Waddington said.

"If he got one and got it in time, no. But we're

runnin' out of time. And there's Crippled Antelope to worry about too. He's got the young men with him, Colonel. My guess is he'll ride back to the village, go into a war dance and ride out with every Hunkpatila he's got with first light."

"Sinte Galeshka can stop him. Kicking Bear can stop his warriors," Waddington said.

"Maybe they can and maybe they can't. Or maybe they won't. I doubt that even Seth can get it called off now."

"Gunn may be right," Seth said. "I kin prob'ly get 'em to sit where they's at for a day or two, but that won't stop them young bucks."

"What in God's name can we do?" Waddington asked.

"There's only one thing where the Hunkpatila warriors are concerned," Gunn said. "I've got a little medicine with them right now, and Crippled Antelope hates me so much he'd put me ahead of anything else — including fighting the Army."

"How can you be so sure of that?" Waddington asked.

"I'm sure," Gunn said. "And if I leave now, I can be back in the village before sunup."

"Looks to me like I ain't ever gonna collect me them two jugs," Seth complained. "You're bitin' off one hell of a big chew."

"Yeah," Gunn observed. "And I may end up swallowing it. You got a better idea?"

Seth shook his head.

"Perhaps if Sinte Galeshka can be convinced we saved him from a trap," Waddington suggested.

"Maybe he'll ride back to the village and confront Crippled Antelope. What do you think, Mister Kinkaid?"

"Well, sir, twixt them bad rifles Gunn talked about, killin' Crow King and the Barker's shenanigans, I'd wager ol' Sinte Galeshka's had about a bellyful of the white man's lies. Don't know if he'd want to believe us or not, but I'm willin' to give it a try."

"And I'll ride with you," the colonel said. "So will the government liaison whether he likes it or not."

"Colonel," Gunn said. "I want you to keep Lisa Briggs with you. Tell her when this is all over—" Gunn paused, considering the possible outcomes—"just tell her I'll see her again."

"I'll tell her," Waddington promised.

Crippled Antelope had seen all he needed to see. Shadow Hand had not lied. He would return to the village and tell what he found. The young men of Sinte Galeshka and Kicking Bear would hear him. They would dance around the council fire, then they would ride with him against the Blue Coats. At his side, protecting him, would be the spirit of the sacred white buffalo, the man called Shadow Hand. He knew now that Shadow Hand was the white man of his vision.

Even as Gunn rode away from Barker's post, Crippled Antelope returned to his village. When he learned that Shadow Hand had escaped and had taken the white girl with him, he went mad with anger. He burned Gunn's sacred tipi, even though the act was in violation of every Sioux law. Finally he went to his own lodge where he found Bright Moon.

Suddenly it came to him, and he realized that she must have helped him escape.

"What do you know of this?" he asked.

"Shadow Hand is protected by the white buffalo. He cannot be killed. He is protected by the blood of his brother, Sinte Galeshka, and he has Tantanka Wakan's war shield."

Crippled Antelope struck her, hard. He stood over her, smiling down at her.

"You carry his seed. You think it is the seed of the white buffalo. I, Crippled Antelope, will kill his seed with mine."

"I will not give myself to you, Crippled Antelope."

"I am not a weakling that you have to give yourself to me," Crippled Antelope said. "I will take you."

The rape of Bright Moon was brutal. Crippled Antelope used his knife to cut the buckskin from her body, and often it ripped into her flesh. He forced himself on her, ripping her with his madness. When it was over she lay bruised and bleeding, but she hadn't cried out, begged for mercy, or whimpered. Even Crippled Antelope felt no victory in his conquest.

When he was through, Crippled Antelope allowed Bright Moon to go to the river, bathe herself and dress. She had just returned to his lodge when they heard the thunder of horses roaring into the village. Crippled Antelope grabbed his rifle, believing it to be the Army. Outside he saw War Eagle, an Oglala Sioux who led the young men of Red Cloud.

"The old chiefs are weak. They squat in the grass like pissing women. Red Cloud sits in council afraid of the white eyes. Sinte Galeshka and Kicking Bear wait to talk to the Blue Coat chief, but I do not wait. My young men have seen many Blue Coats camped along the Niobrara. Will you go with me, Crippled Antelope?"

"Yeeeehooo, hooo, hooo," Crippled Antelope screamed his war cry and fired his rifle into the night sky. "I will lead the Hunkpatila and we will ride with you, War Eagle."

The village was uncommonly dark. A single fire still flickered on the central lodge circle, but only red coals could be seen at other locations. Gunn was puzzled. He held Esquire to a walk.

As he rode through the outside circle of tipis, he realized they were empty. The young men were gone. He urged Esquire into a trot, riding past the inner circle. He saw old Bear sitting by the fire, smoking his pipe. A young woman bared her breast to feed her infant. Walking Tree, his back humped and his gnarled hands held over his head, did his nightly dance around a dying fire.

Gunn dismounted at the tipi of Crippled Antelope and peered in. It was empty. He turned and looked both ways along the line of the council lodges. There was no life.

Gunn saw One Winged Hawk. The young man, barely thirty, was held in special esteem by the Sioux. He had been born deformed, his left arm but a stub. It was believed the spirit of his missing arm guided the Hunkpatila to victories over their enemies.

One Winged Hawk glanced up and raised his arm. "You seek Crippled Antelope?"

"Yes."

"You will fight him?"

"Not if I can help it." Gunn motioned with his hand and looked around again. "Where are they? Where did the young men go?"

"They have gone to kill the Blue Coats. They danced and made big medicine." The Indian waved his arm in a sweeping motion. "Strong medicine. Tatanka Wakan sent them War Eagle and Many Coups and Hump Back Bear to ride with them."

"When?" Gunn asked anxiously. "When did they ride out?"

"The moon was there when they left. Now it is here."

"Which way did they go?"

"Toward the sun's evening house."

"Shit. How many warriors?"

"Many," One Winged Hawk said.

Gunn was about to mount up when he heard someone call him. He looked around to see Deer Spirit.

"Shadow Hand, Crippled Antelope pushed himself into Bright Moon's blankets. She is bleeding but he doesn't think of that. He has dressed her in the hide of the sacred buffalo and he will stake her to the ground. The warriors will touch their weapons to her body as they ride to kill the pony soldiers."

"Did you know where they went?" Gunn asked.

The girl shook her head. "I heard War Eagle speak of the Niobrara."

Gunn mounted. He knew that much from Seth

Kinkaid. The question was, where on the Niobrara?

"This night," Deer Spirit said, "I have seen Crippled Antelope defy the words of Sinte Galeshka and shun the Shaman's vision. He has angered Tatanka Wakan and I have seen, in my dream, blood running red on the sacred buffalo. It is a bad sign."

Gunn rode hell-bent for leather out of the village and due west. He wasn't sure where he was going.

And worse, he feared what he'd find when he got there.

# Chapter Twenty-two

Sinte Galeshka and Kicking Bear were surprisingly receptive. Nonetheless, time was wasted with tradition. They would neither speak about nor hear anything until Colonel Waddington, the liaison, Lieutenant Yardley and Seth Kinkaid had smoked the council pipe with them. The entire business had eaten up nearly an hour. Finally, when all the trappings were taken care of, Sinte Galeshka invited the white men to speak.

"I am speaking from my heart to you, Sinte Galeshka, and to you, Kicking Bear. The medicine for the council meeting is bad. It was a white man who made it bad."

The two chiefs spoke to one another and there were murmurs among the other Indians. Finally, Kicking Bear spoke.

"Did you bring this white man to us?"

"No. He's dead. He was killed by a man you know and trust." Waddington pointed to Seth. "He was killed by this man."

"Who is the man you killed, Great Bear?"

"The man called Barker," Seth said. "He wanted the meetin' at his place, but he was plannin' to set a trap."

"But now he is dead," Sinte Galeshka said. "So there will be no trouble."

"I wish I could say yes to that, Sinte Galeshka," Waddington replied. "But I just can't. Great Bear and the man you call Shadow Hand stopped the trouble here, today, but there is more. Bad trouble and bad medicine."

"Shadow Hand was here today?" Sinte Galeshka said. "But how is this possible?"

"I don't know, but he was there," Seth said. "I seen 'im and talked to 'im."

"What was the plan of Barker?"

The two chiefs listened to the story and learned how they were to be arrested, their village attacked and their people placed on the reservation. Sinte Galeshka finally raised his arm.

"You, Waddington. Would you have come to my village?"

Josiah nodded. "I am a soldier, Sinte Galeshka. I am sworn to my chief as your warriors are sworn to you."

"But you are a soldier chief."

"In the white man's world there are many chiefs," Josiah said. "I am but a small chief and must do what the larger chiefs say. But I would not kill your women and children. And I would fight you only when it was necessary, and I would see to it that you had food and clothing and that white men did not come onto your land."

"This," Kicking Bear said, with a sweep of his arm. "All this was once the land of the Lakota. But you did not stop the white man's wagons, you built forts and you did not hunt down the bad white men, only the bad Lakota."

"That is true, but I, too, have been told lies. Now, I speak from my heart. There is a soldier chief who is bigger than I am, one who wears two stars. He has many soldiers under him and he's waiting to the west of your village. Shadow Hand has gone back to warn your village, to talk to Crippled Antelope. Will you ride there tonight to stop the killing?"

"We will talk of this," Sinte Galeshka said.

"There isn't much time," Waddington cautioned.

"And don't forget about Red Cloud," Seth spoke up. "I seen him comin' north with a heap o' warriors. Sinte Galeshka, I know you got somethin' planned, but it ain't gonna work. They's just too damn many soldiers."

Seth's words took the chiefs by surprise. It was as though he was a Shaman with a vision of their plan.

"Wait," Kicking Bear said. "We will speak of this."

Seth, Waddington and the others retired a discreet distance away from the council fire while the Indians talked. Seth took a bite from his plug, then offered it to Colonel Waddington, who joined him.

"Mister Kinkaid, I'm afraid you were right. If the blood bath is going to be stopped, Gunn's going to have to do it."

"Seems thataway, Colonel." Seth wallowed his chew from one cheek to the other and then spat. "But I'm thinkin' the only way he'll get that job done is to send Crippled Antelope to the happy huntin' ground."

An hour passed, then two. The young lieutenant was snoring, Colonel Waddington had been dozing fitfully and Seth Kinkaid was as asleep as he ever got. Suddenly Seth sat bolt upright. His movement awakened the others.

"Kinkaid?" Waddington said. "What is it?"

Seth stood up and looked toward the council fire. It was burned down now to a few glowing embers.

"They're gone," Seth said.

"What? What are you talkin' about?"

"The Injuns. They've hightailed it outa here."

"That's not possible," the lieutenant said. "They couldn't have left without one of us hearing."

"Boy, from the way you was snorin', they could marched out behind a brass band and you wouldn't knowed it. I can't be talkin' none, though, 'cause I let 'em go just like you did."

"Why, Kinkaid?" Waddington asked. "Why would they sneak out on us like that?"

"My guess is they rode off to meet Red Cloud. They'll prob'ly spend most of tomorrow palaverin' with him. Won't be long after that till we'll know what they got planned."

"Damn!" Waddington said.

"Well, sir, if'n it'll make you feel any better, Colonel, they would'na rode off if'n they hadn't believed what you tol' 'em."

"Thank you, Kinkaid, but that's damned little consolation. Let's get mounted, gentlemen. We're going back to camp, then I'm taking the troops back to Fort Randall."

"We're going back tonight, sir?"

"Yes, Lieutenant, we are. If Gunn is as unsuccessful with his mission as we have been with ours, we must be ready to retaliate against the Sioux at once."

"Yes, sir."

"Kinkaid, I know you came out here on your own. But I could really use a man like you. Will you ride with us?"

Seth spat, chewed a moment and spat again. "Reckon I can do that," he said. "Got one question naggin' at me, though."

"What's that?"

"This here retaliatin' you talkin' about."

"Yes?"

"You figurin' on doin' that before or after the buryin'?"

## Chapter Twenty-three

Fog slithered along every creek, dry wash and low spot as Gunn neared the Niobrara. Dawn had come on the heels of a prairie thunderstorm, short but furious, with raindrops as large as two-bit pieces. Now the air was heavy, clinging to horse and man like an invisible, soaked shroud.

Gunn's eyes burned from lack of sleep and his lower back felt as if he'd been kicked by a mule. His butt throbbed from constant contact with the saddle. He couldn't remember the last full night's sleep he'd had and his thinking processes were so muddled that he could only concentrate in short spurts. It was no shape to be in and he knew it. The worst thing that could happen to him now would be to run, headlong, into Crippled Antelope.

He slipped from Esquire's back and they walked together to the river. Gunn dropped his gunbelt along the water's edge, removed his shirt and boots and waded out 'til the river was chest deep. He submerged himself several times, bathed his face repeatedly, then returned to shore. He dropped into the grass.

How long he had slept he didn't know. He sat up, rubbed his eyes and got to his feet. From the sun he figured that it was about seven-thirty. He knew there was little chance he had accomplished anything by riding all night. His only hope was the Army's fixation with schedules and regimentation. Even with the added warriors, Gunn doubted that Crippled Antelope would attack a full cavalry regiment. He was guessing that Crippled Antelope and War Eagle would split up into two forces, not only as a matter of tactics, but, Indianlike, as a way to preserve the individual integrity of the battle.

Gunn rode due north. By the description of Seth's meeting with the Fifth, he should at least be able to see their breakfast fires. He was certain they'd have them, since the last thing they'd be expecting was an attack. He'd ridden less than five miles when he saw the smoke. He stopped, and patted Esquire's neck.

"Sure as hell isn't a campfire," he said. The smoke was thick and black. He rode to the top of a hill. The slope to its summit was gradual and it took him several minutes to negotiate it. The scene below him was self-explanatory.

The Foster place had been there for several years. Harvey Foster had been a Reb during the late war, but harbored no ill will against anyone, Yankee or Indian.

Gunn found his body draped across the hitching rail in front of the main house, a tomahawk still buried in his back. Ellie Foster looked asleep. She was propped against a tree alongside her two daughters. All three of them had bullet holes through their foreheads. Ellie's death grip still held the Colt. The only Foster son, Hank, was in the Army. Gunn had heard that he was posted at Fort Riley, down in Kansas.

Gunn hated not being able to bury them, but there was no time. Clearly the Sioux were on a rampage of death. Until they found the Army any white man, woman or child was fair game. He rode hard now. His eyes no longer burned, but the anger in his gut blazed like a coal furnace.

The shot was close enough for Gunn to hear it split the air. He crouched low and dug his spurs into Esquire's sides. The horse seemed to find more strength in those powerful legs. Gunn turned his head enough to catch a glimpse of his antagonist. Three—no, four. Another head appeared. Five. Five Sioux bucks, breaking off from the main body, striking whenever and wherever they could find a target.

Esquire barely slowed down as they reached the stand of trees. Gunn pulled the Winchester from its sheath and jumped from the horse's back almost in a single motion. It was a move made only by a man with plenty of experience doing it. The ground was soft and Gunn stayed on his feet. He spotted a log. He dived and was in the prone position, at the ready, when the first two Indians rode into view.

Two shots, two dead Sioux! Their horses veered off and ran by him. Bark flew from the log and he heard it tick his hat. He swung the Winchester's barrel three inches to the left and squeezed off another shot. The big warrior's head jerked and his body was lifted from the horse's back. The others let out war whoops as they rode by. Both fired, but neither shot was close.

Gunn got to his feet. Esquire had already circled and

came trotting out of the trees. The Sioux had topped a nearby ridge. They sat, side by side, looking down. Gunn could have dropped at least one of them, a hell of a shot, but one he could handle. He didn't. They rode toward him, shortening the distance between them. When it became a hundred yards, Gunn was ready.

Gunn had followed the one on the left carefully. Now, he locked in on him. The Winchester bucked against Gunn's shoulder. The Indian had just squeezed his legs together for the final charge. The .44 slug broke the brave's breastbone and carried him tumbling off the back of his horse. Gunn darted into the stand of trees, mounted up and charged out, up the hill, toward the one remaining Indian.

The Indian turned his pony and rode out of sight. It was exactly what Gunn had wanted. He had his track to the main body.

Maj. Gen. Armstead Tucker Hawes was only forty-four years old. He had prematurely white hair, but his beard was as black as coal. During the war he had commanded a special unit of cavalry, charged with the destruction of railroads and bridges behind southern lines. While he had been breveted twice, he never received the public acclaim in the North that men like John Hunt Morgan or Nathan Bedford Forrest received in the South for doing the same thing. At the war's conclusion he asked for and received permission to come west. Here, he hoped, he would gain the acclaim he was due.

After the meeting with Seth Kinkaid, the Fifth had turned due north. Hawes split his force, but there were only five miles between the two columns. He was hoping for an attack against one of the columns by Indians, any Indians.

Hawes took personal command of the westernmost column and assigned Col. Delahunt Mosby to the eastern column. Mosby was a cousin of the famed Virginia Confederate raider, John S. Mosby. Hawes never felt more confident than he did at this moment. Nearly every man wearing the Fifth's insignia was a veteran campaigner. Many had experience both in the Civil War and against the Indians.

The two forces camped that night along the Rosebud. Hawes set up his field headquarters, then called for a staff meeting.

"Gentlemen," he began. "The future of America's western empire may very well rest on the outcome of this campaign. We have the element of surprise among our weapons, and the official sanction of some of the most important leaders in Washington. Those facts, combined with the skills and experience of this force, will prove more than adequate to the task it faces. Now, to specifics."

The hand of a young lieutenant went up. Hawes was visibly irritated.

"Yes, Lieutenant?"

"Begging the general's pardon, sir, but aren't we here to assure the compliance of the Sioux to any agreements reached by Colonel Waddington?"

"Lieutenant, your query is out of order. Colonel Waddington acted on his own to set up a council with the Indians. The fact is, political considerations take precedence over the personal desires of a field commander." He paused and added a rather cynical footnote. "Particularly when that commander holds only the rank of lieutenant-colonel."

The lieutenant glanced around at the others. He knew he was alone in his protest.

"Does that answer your question, Lieutenant?"

"Uh, yes, sir. Thank you, sir."

"Good. Now, tomorrow, Colonel Mosby will lead his six companies north to the White River." Hawes pulled a blanket away from an easel to reveal a rather detailed map of the area. "He will bivouac here." He pointed to a spot fifteen miles from the suspected location of the Hunkpatila village, then turned to Mosby. "You will retain one company in reserve. A second should be sent east as far as the Missouri to discourage any attempt by the hostiles to escape in that direction."

"Yes, sir. How will we maintain communication?"

Hawes smiled broadly. "Always a problem in this country, Colonel, but not tomorrow. I intend that we should use a pony express system. I will supply three riders and so will you. None have far to go and the relay system will ensure rapid delivery of field orders."

"Excellent, sir!"

"Yes," Hawes said. "Isn't it? Now, then, when we have received word of the outcome of the council, we will move at once. If the Sioux have agreed to move, we will simply encircle the village and await the return of the chiefs. If they agree to move to the reservation, we will escort them."

"And if they haven't agreed?" Mosby asked.

"In that case, instead of merely surrounding the village, we will attack. You, Colonel, from the north. I want no skirmish lines, no defensive posture. It is to be a full cavalry charge by three troops."

"Yes, sir."

"I will time a similar charge with all my units, save the reserve company, once your men have cleared the village. Additional action by the remainder of your forces will be dictated by circumstance. Questions?" Hawes looked directly at the young lieutenant. The lieutenant swallowed hard and shifted his eyes, but said nothing. Neither did anyone else. "Very well. Sleep soundly, gentlemen."

The Fifth had moved farther north than either Gunn or Crippled Antelope had guessed. The big Sioux had spotted them headed north, but anticipated their rate of movement would place them in camp some ten miles south of their actual location. Dawn brought disappointment. Many of the young braves, too riled and too anxious for action, broke away from the main body. The Fosters had been victims of one such band. Four others had fallen victim to Gunn's Winchester.

Crippled Antelope called a halt to his own line of march about eight-thirty. He sat down with War Eagle.

"The Blue Coats have gone there," he said, pointing north. "We must send riders to find them, then we will attack from two sides."

"My young men become restless. Some say they have seen bad signs. Others run away to find whites and kill them. If we do not fight soon, more will run away."

"Can you not control your braves?" Crippled Antelope asked angrily. "Speak to them. Tell them to have patience. Soon we will find the Blue Coats."

War Eagle stood and nodded, then he said, "I think if we do not find them when the sun is highest, many will not fight."

Crippled Antelope stood also. "We will find them. We will fight before the sun is high."


Including the supply company, Indian scouts and muleskinners, the Fifth cavalry had 627 men in the field. The combined forces of War Eagle and Crippled Antelope totalled nearly twice that number. Crippled Antelope knew he had a distinct advantage but with each passing hour he could feel victory slipping away.

The warriors milled about, mumbling, occasionally arguing loudly among themselves. Only when they saw a war party of nearly twenty-five men ride north did some calm prevail. Crippled Antelope sat alone. He opened a buckskin pouch and dumped its contents on the ground in front of him. He stared down at the teeth of the white buffalo.

He looked into the future and shuddered.

# Chapter Twenty-four

Gunn saw the Sioux warrior's pony disappear over a hill. Then his eyes refocused on the deep-blue shade of the sky beyond. It wasn't blue anymore. It was tinted with a weak shade of reddish-orange. Dust! Gunn spurred Esquire on until he reached the summit of the hill.

"Damn!" he said aloud as he sat on the top of the hill and looked down into the valley below. The warrior he had been tracking was gone, lost in a dust storm raised by hundreds of Indian ponies and their riders. The seething mass of Indians was moving like a plague of locusts off to the northeast. Gunn would have to outride them. He looked west for the edge of the dust cloud.

Esquire's muscles rippled and the big horse's mane was nearly flat against his neck, held in place by the wind. Gunn sat low in the saddle, reducing the friction, giving Esquire his head. Down, down he rode until he cleared the dust, then he turned north.

They crossed a stream, throwing up a spray of water

to flash silver in the sun. Hooves cracked against rocks and flanks grew frothy with sweat as Esquire pulled hill after hill. Another stream, wider than the one before. A rocky slope with a sliding surface so that climbing the hill took three steps for every two gained. Esquire reached the top, his great sides heaving from the strain. Gunn pulled up.

"Easy," he said. "Take it easy, boy."

Esquire trotted, then Gunn swung down and they walked. Finally they stopped and Gunn looked down at the grasslands spread before them. It was flat, with gentle undulations.

This land ran north across the Dakota Territories all the way to Canada. It was the land of the Brule, the Teton, the Minneconjous, the Oglala and the Hunkpatila. Here, only a decade ago, the buffalo were too numerous to be counted. Now, few could be found. Within another decade Gunn knew there would be fence lines, plowed fields, grazing cattle and railroads. He wasn't sure he approved of it, but he understood its inevitability. He turned east and rode another half hour. He knew the mass of Sioux would be moving only a third as fast as he.

"Lone rider, sir," a young sentry called. His lieutenant walked to the edge of the encampment.

"Looks like a white man," the lieutenant said.

The sentry lowered his rifle as Gunn approached.

"Where you bound for, mister?" the lieutenant asked.

"To see your commanding officer," Gunn said. He

looked around for a guidon. "This is the Fifth?"

"Yes, sir. Lieutenant Thomas Finely, sir, D Troop, United States Fifth Cavalry out of Fort Sedgewick."

"Who is your commanding officer, Lieutenant?"

"Major General Hawes, sir."

"Take me to him, please. I'm scout William Gunnison, here on Army business."

"Yes, sir, follow me."

Gunn looked around at the men. They were restless, edgy, like men before a battle.

"Guess you'd be the dispatch rider now, wouldn't you?" the lieutenant asked. "The man from the council between the Sioux and Colonel Waddington. Didn't look for you to be ridin' in from the west."

Gunn didn't answer. They'd reached General Hawes. The general looked up in question as they arrived.

"Here's our man, General," the lieutenant said. "Rode in from the west."

"Why in thunder did you waste all the time to circle around to the west, man?" General Hawes asked irritably. "If we lose the element of surprise, it's going to make this campaign much more difficult. Now, tell me, sir, what is the verdict?"

"I'd like the speak to you in private, General."

"In private? What in thunder for? Who the hell are you?"

"Not who you're expectin'," Gunn said. "Nevertheless, we'd best talk." Gunn walked away for several yards, then turned back. The general was staring, angered by the man's arrogance and demand. Finally he walked over to him.

"All right, what's this all about, mister? And it had better be good, damn good. I'm not used to being summoned by a scout in front of my own men."

"General, my name is Gunn. I know all about your orders, where they came from, who instigated them and why. You've already lost the element of surprise." Gunn pointed to the southeast. "Somewhere out there, not too damned far, are more than a thousand Sioux warriors. If you don't get your ass out of here now, you won't have a regiment by noon." Gunn looked back toward the troopers. "As a matter of fact, it doesn't appear to me that you have an entire regiment here, now."

"The remaining six troops are five miles west and about fifteen miles north of here, though that is certainly none of your concern. I don't know who you think you represent, Mister Gunn, but I will not formulate military tactics on your say-so."

The general's revelation about the split force brought a knot to Gunn's stomach. The Sioux could destroy them all the more easily now.

"Why the hell won't you formulate tactics on my say-so? I'm a scout. What the hell are scouts for if not to give commanders the information they need?"

"You may be a scout, sir, but you are not my scout," General Hawes said. "I see no reason why I should take your word on this."

"Then don't take my word, General. Mount a patrol and I'll give you all the proof you need."

"Give me one reason why I should."

"One? Why you pompous son of a bitch, send a patrol with me and I'll give you a thousand." Gunn started toward his horse.

"Sentry, stop that man!" General Hawes shouted.

Gunn's Colt appeared from nowhere. He leveled it at the general. "Mount the patrol, General, now!"

"Mister, you have pulled a gun on the United States Army."

Gunn squeezed the trigger and the general's hat flew off. The bullet nipped through his hair, barely missing his scalp.

"I'm running a might short on patience, General, and you're running square out of time. Now, mount the patrol."

The general authorized a six-man patrol to mount and a moment later Gunn and the six men headed east. They had ridden less than two miles when they saw a body of two or three dozen Indians. They were badly outnumbered, so they rode quickly back to the camp. The Indians followed, but drew no closer than a nearby ridge line. Gunn pointed them out to the general.

"Do you see them, General, over on the ridge?"

"I see them, Mister Gunn. By my count, no more than thirty. Hardly a reason to flee in panic."

"Don't be a damned fool," Gunn said. "You think thirty Indians would come this close to us if they weren't backed up by hundreds more? They're just scouts, that's all." Suddenly Gunn felt the hardness of a rifle barrel pressed into the middle of his back. The general grinned.

"Good job, trooper. Now, disarm him. You, Mister Gunn, are under arrest. For the moment I will call it detention, rather than arrest. And if there is a larger body of hostiles about, I'll consider that in my report concerning your actions."

"Gen'rul, sir," one of the men shouted. "Rider comin'. Looks to be one of our men."

A moment later a trooper reached them. He struggled to bring his mount under control and when he dismounted, his face showed concern and fear.

"What is it?" General Hawes said.

"They must be a thousand or more of 'em, Gen'rul," he said. "And somethin' else, they're all ridin' together."

"What do you mean?"

"Sioux, Crow, Cheyenne, ridin' side by side like they was all brothers. They got us hemmed in, Gen'rul. I barely got through."

The Sioux war party on the ridge turned and rode out of sight. One of the troopers nearby suddenly let out a choked call.

"God almighty, look!" he said, pointing to the north.

Just to the north of the encampment the prairie sloped into a shallow valley and ran in a gentle upgrade to a long, low ridge. The ridge was easily a mile long, running from northeast to southwest. Upon it, for its entire length, on spotted and painted ponies, sat mounted warriors.

"Son of a bitch," Gunn said. With the soldiers distracted by the appearance of so many Indians, Gunn used the opportunity to jerk the rifle away from the trooper who was guarding him. Then he pulled his pistol and jammed it into General Hawes' belly.

"What? What are you doing?" the general gasped.

"Like as not I'd be doin' you a favor if I blew a hole in you right now," Gunn said.

"I suppose I did react somewhat hastily," Hawes said

Gunn put his pistol away. "I'll make a deal. You don't point any more guns at me and I won't point any more at you."

"All right," Hawes agreed, nervously.

Gunn looked toward the south. There was a fringe of dust along the horizon. "The other half," he said pointing. "You ever fight Indians, General?"

"Of course I have."

"Good! That might help keep some of you alive long enough for me to bring you some help."

"Help?"

"The rest of your regiment. You were a fool to divide them like this. Your only chance now is to bring the entire regiment together for this fight. And you'll still be badly outnumbered. I'm going after them."

"That won't be necessary," General Hawes said. "I have a most efficient relay system stretching between this force and my troops to the north. Six riders. Why they can cover the distance in no more than half an hour."

"Beggin' your pardon, Gen'rul," the trooper who just rode in said. "But you ain't got them no more."

"What are you talking about?"

"They're dead, Gen'rul. Ever'one of 'em."

Hawes' face paled. He looked at Gunn, his expression blank. He was already a defeated man.

"Get your men ready for a fight, General," Gunn said. "I'll try and reach the others in time." Gunn climbed onto Esquire and spurred him into a gallop to the northeast.

"They won't let him through," Hawes said. "Not i

they killed our men."

"I don't think he figures they'll let him through, Gen'rul," a nearby sergeant said. "But he's got a pretty good way o' distractin' them while he tries."

"Oh? And what way is that, Sergeant?"

The sergeant grinned. "Why, us, sir," he answered.

# Chapter Twenty-five

Even as Gunn left General Hawes and his men, Colonel Waddington had stripped Fort Randall of its defenses. He left behind less than one company of troopers with orders to abandon the fort and escort the women and children to the east if an attack appeared imminent. The remaining force marched into the field at eleven o'clock, minus Seth Kinkaid.

In a last-minute change of plans, Waddington asked Kinkaid to ride back to the camp of Red Cloud and try to encourage the combined Indian forces to disband. The colonel believed he could argue successfully against the original orders given to the Fifty Cavalry only if he could show that the major chiefs were acting responsibly. Waddington had a long march ahead of him but he intended to ride only as far as the Hunkpatila village. There, he would rendezvous with Kinkaid and, he hoped, Sinte Galeshka and Kicking Bear.

Seth had been right about the two chief's destination. He found them in council with Red Cloud and the other chiefs when he arrived on the Rosebud. He was welcomed with less enthusiasm this time.

"I come to palaver ag'in," he said. "No promises, no treaty, just tryin' to keep a heap o' folks from dyin', white and red."

"The talk is empty," Sinte Galeshka said. "The young men of many tribes have already joined together. By now many pony soldiers have died."

"Yo're likely right about that," Seth said. "But they's still all o' you. If them young bucks wiped out most o' the cavalry, the next soldiers what ride out this way won't pay no mind to what Injuns they kill. Like as not, they'll just commence to killin'."

"We are only old men, women and children here, Great Bear. The soldiers would not attack us. We have no warriors — we are no danger to them."

"Do you not remember Sand Creek? Washita? Did the soldiers not kill old men, women and children in those places?"

"You speak from the heart, Great Bear, and with a straight tongue," Kicking Bear said. He stood up. "I will lead my Hunkpatila away from the land, north to the land of the Grandmother. I hope my young men will come with us."

"I, too, will lead my people away from here," Sinte Galeshka said. "My heart is sick and I tire of talking. My heart hurts for my dead brothers."

American Horse stood up next and indicated that he, too, would leave. All eyes turned to Red Cloud. The old chief was silent for a moment, then he turned to face the others.

"Hear me. The young ones do not know how much

we have seen, how much we have suffered. When I look back now from this high hill of old age I can see women and children killed and scattered through the land. I can see the spirits of the Indian people who have died in the bloody mud. The sacred hoop is broken now. There is no center anymore. I will lead my people from this place."

"That there is the smart thing to do," Seth said. "You've all showed a heap of smart."

Red Cloud looked at Seth sadly. "We will leave, Great Bear, but the blood will flow again. Crazy Horse, Rain In The Face, Gall, Two Moon, Hump, many others in the land of Greasy Grass will fight. They are led by the great Shaman, Sitting Bull. In a vision, Sitting Bull saw that there would be a big fight and all the Blue Coats would die."

"You don't believe that, do you? That all the soldiers could be killed?"

"Yes," Red Cloud said. "Sitting Bull has great medicine."

"If'n that does happen, there will be more soldiers come than ever before," Seth said.

"Yes," Red Cloud said. "This, I know." Red Cloud made a sweeping motion with his arms and, instantly the Indians began dismantling tipis and loading their travois. In a matter of minutes the village was broken up and they were on their way. Soon, there would be no sign of them. They were headed home, home to the Republican River country.

Seth caught up with Waddington about midway between Barker's post and the Hunkpatila village.

"Well?"

"I done it, Colonel. Red Cloud's headin' south, Sinte Galeshka and Kicking Bear are goin' north."

"Thank God."

"That don't say nothin' for them fellas in the Fifth, though. They's still a heap o' Injuns out there 'n' they're the fightin' kind."

"Perhaps Gunn can stop them."

"That's a tall order, even for him, Colonel."

"Yes, I know." Waddington frowned and rubbed the back of his neck. He removed his hat and mopped his brow, then looked at Seth. "You have any idea of the repercussions, the revenge that would result from the destruction of an entire cavalry regiment?"

"Ain't never pondered on it, Colonel."

"It must never happen.

At that very moment Gunn was considering the very possibility of a cavalry regiment being destroyed. He had ridden hard for eight miles. There was another gently sloping hill ahead of him and from there, he thought, he would be able to see the camp of the remaining forces of the Fifth Cavalry.

At the top of the hill he saw not the remaining troops, but more than a hundred Indians. They saw him as well and several warriors started toward him. Suddenly they stopped. The head of a white horse came into view, then its rider. His right arm was held high. In his hand he gripped a rifle.

"So, you have come to die with the Blue Coats, Shadow Hand?"

"No," Gunn said. "I have come to kill you, Crippled

Antelope. You have spoken with two tongues to your brother, War Eagle. You are buffalo dung who fights women. You have angered Tatanka Wakan and angered the spirit of the white buffalo."

I wonder if they're buyin' this bullshit, Gunn thought. He had no idea if what he was saying was getting through, but when he saw the expression of anger on Crippled Antelope's face he knew his words were having some effect.

"When the valley runs with the blood of the Blue Coats, I will cut out your tongue for those words," Crippled Antelope sneered.

"You think you can kill the soldiers while the spirit of the white buffalo lives in me?" Gunn laughed. "There's only one way you can know victory, Crippled Antelope, and that is to defeat me in battle. But you will not fight me, for you have the heart of a coward. You fight only women who cannot fight back."

Gunn's words had a little more effect this time, not so much with Crippled Antelope as with the others around him. Gunn smiled. He hoped to make Crippled Antelope lose enough face that he would be forced to fight.

Crippled Antelope trotted his pony sideways for a few paces, then he motioned with his arm and two warriors carried up a stake. It was fashioned like a cross and tied to it by strips of rawhide, showing the bruises of her beating, was Bright Moon. She was naked and her head was rolling from side to side. She was alive.

Crippled Antelope laughed. "You are a Christian man, Gunn. Here is your Christian sign. I have stolen your Christian medicine and I have stolen the seed of the white buffalo which you put in her body. Now the medicine is mine."

Gunn rode closer and noticed that some of the warriors backed off. He rode still closer and others moved. They split apart. Crippled Antelope looked both ways. For the first time, he was showing some concern.

"You don't have shit, Crippled Antelope. I was your prisoner and you couldn't kill me, so you took it out on a woman. Sinte Galeshka sent her to me the first time, but the second time she came on her own. You say she was your woman? She was never your woman, because you aren't a man."

Gunn noticed that a few more warriors were putting some distance between themselves and Crippled Antelope. He was gaining some ground.

Gunn slipped from Esquire's back, picked up a stick and drew a line into the dirt.

"This is the line that keeps you from attacking the soldiers. The warriors will not fight them until the white buffalo spirit is yours and you have the war shield." He stepped back, pointed south and drew a deep breath. If this didn't work, he was a dead man.

"Well, go ahead, Crippled Antelope. See if I speak with two tongues. Order the attack, if you can."

The next ten seconds were the longest of Gunn's life. Then the warriors scattered. War Eagle appeared. His hand was held high.

"I have heard your words, Shadow Hand. And I have heard the words of Crippled Antelope. Who speaks the truth? You will fight Crippled Antelope. If you lie, Crippled Antelope will kill you."

"And if I kill Crippled Antelope, will you call off the war?"

"I will speak of it to my warriors. I will go with you to speak of it to the Blue Coats."

Crippled Antelope rode over and grabbed War Eagle by the arm.

"Wait! Don't listen to the words of Shadow Hand! The Blue Coats are in our circle, they—" War Eagle pulled free.

"I will not speak of this thing to you," War Eagle said. "Do you tremble at the words of Shadow Hand? Is it you who speaks with two tongues?"

War Eagle turned and rode toward Gunn. Just as the Indian reached Gunn, there was a rifle shot. War Eagle turned and looked back toward Crippled Antelope, who was holding his rifle, barrel pointed up. Smoke was curling from the end of the barrel.

"Look upon this thing," Crippled Antelope screamed. "See the death of the white buffalo's spirit and the woman of Shadow Hand!"

Bright Moon's eyes grew big. She tugged at her bonds, but she didn't cry out. Crippled Antelope thrust his lance into her, just below her navel. A stream of blood gushed down.

"You rotten bastard!" Gunn called, slipping his rifle from its sheath. War Eagle was close enough to him now to grab the barrel and he did so.

"No!" he said. "You cannot kill him this way. You must fight him. It is the test."

Gunn's brain was on fire. He felt the hate spreading through him like raw liquor, infecting him, heating his blood, exploding in his mind. He remembered Bright Moon's warm, young body against his own, her touch, her softness.

"God damn him!" Gunn shouted. He felt War Eagle's grip tighten on the rifle. He looked into the warrior's face and saw understanding, even some pain. Gunn nodded weakly.

"Come," War Eagle said. "We will speak to the Blue Coats."

"What if Crippled Antelope decides to attack while we are talking?"

War Eagle turned and called something over his shoulder. Half the warriors moved out of line.

"If Crippled Antelope tries to lead his young men, my young men will fight them," he said.

"All right, War Eagle. Let's go," Gunn said.


It had been a day of surprises for Armstead Tucker Hawes. He had expected an immediate attack, but it didn't come. The circle of Indians tightened around him, but still the attack didn't come.

"General," a nearby lieutenant called to him. The lieutenant was looking through field glasses. "Here comes Gunn."

"Gunn is returning? Without Mosby's men?"

"Yes, sir. Fact is . . ." The lieutenant stopped. "I don't understand this, General."

"What is it, man? What don't you understand?"

"There's an Indian riding alongside Gunn. Looks like they're coming in to talk."

"If that son of a bitch has negotiated a surrender I'll

have him executed," General Hawes swore.

A moment later Gunn and War Eagle reached the encampment. Gunn dismounted but War Eagle stayed on his horse, looking around with brown, expressionless eyes at the soldiers who were staring back at him.

"What's going on here, mister?" General Hawes demanded. "What have you done? Whatever deal you have made I cancel. I'm placing you and this Indian under arrest right now."

Gunn shut the general up with a solid punch to the chin. The general went down like a sack of flour.

A couple of men started toward Gunn but he stopped them by drawing his pistol. He looked around and saw one old private watching on, stoically.

"Tapley?" he said.

"That's me, Gunn," the private answered.

"What are you doing here? I thought you were with Waddington."

"I was," Tapley said. "Wish to hell I still was, but when another general come into the area, why my brother just naturally had to assign me here to keep him up with what's goin' on."

"Yeah, well, don't pack it in yet, Tapley, but if we get lucky, we may be headed home by supper time. I've got a fight to finish. If I win, it's over."

"That's the good part, Gunn. What if you lose?" Tapley asked.

"It'll still be over," he said. "It'll just take a little longer, that's all."

Tapley pointed to the general, who was just now sitting up, rubbing his chin.

"I reckon he'll be writin' that up in his field report,"

Tapley said. "Like as not it'll take up more space than the whole battle."

"What do you figure I'll get for hittin' him, Tapley? A fine, or some time in the stockade? Or both."

"Prob'ly both," Tapley said. "Though if it was up to me, you'd get a medal."

Gunn looked out across the field toward the hundreds and hundreds of warriors who had them surrounded.

"Time in the stockade, huh? Not a pleasant prospect," he said. He laughed then, the first sincere laugh he had enjoyed in days.

Since bivouacking the night before, Colonel Mosby had kept small patrols in the field constantly. Twice, one of them had ridden to where they could see the north end of the Hunkpatila village. Now, Mosby was uneasy. It was nearing two o'clock. His men had not seen any signs of the relay riders, nor had they seen any Indians.

"Lieutenant, I want you to take twenty-five men to General Hawes. We should have heard something by now."

"Sir," the lieutenant replied, pointing. "It seems we're about to." The last patrol Mosby had ordered out was returning at the gallop.

"You've seen the hostiles?" Mosby asked.

"No, sir, Army! Looks like about eight companies, maybe more. They were riding into the Indian village."

"Attacking?"

"No, sir! Rode in real peacefullike. Not a shot,

nothing, sir. I think they're the troops from Fort Randall."

"Lieutenant, when you rendezvous with General Hawes, take him this messsage," Mosby said. He scribbled out a dispatch and jammed it into the lieutenant's hand. "Bring me his reply."

"Yes, sir. Where will you be?"

"In that village."

"Yes, sir."

Seth Kinkaid had ridden only part of the way with Colonel Waddington's column. After they talked about it, they decided that Seth should ride on ahead, beyond the village, and scout the territory for signs of a battle, the Fifth, Indians or Gunn. Seth cleared the last obstacle, then came upon them.

Seth had never seen anything quite like the scene spread below him. Besides being in awe of the numbers involved, he was puzzled as to the Indians' relaxed demeanor. He rode toward the circle, searching for the lances which would signify the location of the chiefs. He found them.

"Howdy, War Eagle," he said.

"Do you bring more Blue Coats, Great Bear?"

"No. They're back a-thataway, at the village of Sinte Galeshka."

"Do they come to fight?"

"No. Sinte Galeshka, Kicking Bear and Red Cloud have made peace." Seth looked around. "You fellas don't look like you're about to fight."

"There will be a fight," War Eagle said. "Soon." War

Eagle recounted the day's events to Seth. Seth nodded.

"I'd be obliged if I could ride down and palaver some with Gunn, uh, Shadow Hand. Like to send a soldier back to the village, too, tell 'em what's goin' on so they don't come chargin' in here without askin' questions."

"Yes," War Eagle said.

"Thanks," Seth said. He found Gunn and told him what had happened in the village. Then he asked the question that was on everyone's mind.

"Can you help that warrior, Gunn?"

"You want to stand in for me, Seth?" Gunn asked, smiling.

"Nope. But I've seen you lookin' a mite more fit."

"This morning, Seth, he would have had the edge. Not now."

"What's different?"

"He killed Bright Moon, killed her with me looking on. I could have stopped it, could've dropped him before he got the job done."

"An' I'da rode into a heap o' dead men," Seth replied.

"Yeah, but right now it doesn't make it any easier."

"That there white girl—" Seth started.

"Lisa?"

Yeah. She wouldn't have no truck stayin' at the fort. She rode in with the colonel."

"Don't tell her what's going on."

"Don't reckon I'll see her to tell her anythin'. War Eagle 'lowed me to ride in, didn't say nothin' 'bout ridin' out. Reckon that's gonna be up to you."

Gunn nodded grimly, then put his hand on Seth's shoulder.

"If I lose, Seth, Crippled Antelope will lead the first

charge. Not even War Eagle will be able to stop him. Colonel Waddington's troops won't make any difference to him."

"I'd say that's about the size of it," Seth agreed.

"Kill him, Seth. If you have to stay out of it 'til you get the bastard, promise me you'll kill him."

"I'll get 'im, Gunn." He raised up the .50 Sharps. "He'll never get to the first line of soldiers, I give you my word on it."

Gunn smiled. "If they've got jugs in the happy hunting grounds, I'll owe you another one."

Seth shook his head. "Nuhn-uh. This here 'un's on old Seth Kinkaid."

# Chapter Twenty-six

All the players were on stage and in their proper positions. The drama was about to unfold.

Colonel Mosby had exchanged information with Colonel Waddington, and both of them had moved onto the theater of war, should battle break out. Neither of them would be present for the fight between Gunn and Crippled Antelope. Neither would Seth Kinkaid or Lisa Briggs. Sinte Galeshka rode to the scene as soon as he heard what was about to happen, and he was there as a witness.

War Eagle was there and so was General Hawes. If nothing else, time had made the odds between the opposing forces more even. Mosby's and Waddington's troops, in support of Hawes' column, meant that the battle would be intense and bloody, with a great loss of life on both sides.

For the fight, both men had agreed that the code of the Lakota would be the rule. Each man would begin the battle fully armed and on horseback. Crippled Antelope would have his rifle, his tomahawk and his knife. Gunn would be armed with his rifle, a tomahawk borrwed from Sinte Galeshka and his own knife.

There would be no violations of the code. If either man acted outside the code, War Eagle would kill him.

Gunn and Crippled Antelope were a hundred yards apart. Esquire was nervous and he pawed at the ground. Gunn talked gently to him. Crippled Antelope cradled his rifle under his arm. In a single motion he could move and fire it.

If Gunn were facing a white gunfighter he would have all the confidence in the world. There he would be in familiar territory. But he wasn't even wearing his pistol for this battle and he knew that Crippled Antelope was at least his equal with a rifle, and much better with tomahawk and knife. Gunn realized he was up against one of the most dangerous opponents he had ever faced.

War Eagle held his lance up above his head, then threw it into the ground. That was the signal to begin.

Esquire reared, then his hind legs dug into the ground and the big horse charged forward. Crippled Antelope's pony responded as well and the distance closed.

Gunn released the reins and hoisted the Winchester to his shoulder. Crippled Antelope's rifle was already in position. Suddenly the big warrior's body slipped to the side. His huge, muscular legs tightened around his mount's girth. He fired. Gunn heard the bullet strike the leather of his saddle, high on the saddle's cantle beneath his buttocks. He felt nothing.

Gunn's steel-blue eyes squinted in the afternoon sun. They were close. Gunn fired. Crippled Antelope winced and pulled himself upright. The rifle flew from his grip, its stock split by Gunn's shot.

Gunn reined up. He turned Esquire. The little

Indian pony was already turned and running hard toward Gunn's position. Crippled Antelope was swinging his tomahawk. He was too close for Gunn to do anything but try and parry the blow with his rifle.

The tomahawk grazed Gunn's left thigh. It felt like the kick of a mule, but it didn't sink itself into his flesh. On the other hand, Gunn managed to catch Crippled Antelope with the butt of his rifle, knocking the warrior from his horse, but losing his rifle in the process. Crippled Antelope groaned, rolled and bounced. Gunn leaped from Esquire's back and slapped the horse to move him away.

Crippled Antelope got to his feet, then began circling with the tomahawk in his right hand, his knife still in the sheath at his side. Gunn raised his tomahawk, though it was obvious he wasn't as comfortable with it as Crippled Antelope. In fact, he looked to see how the Indian was holding the tomahawk so he could hold his the same way.

Crippled Antelope realized the advantage was now his, and he smiled broadly.

"Tell me, Shadow Hand, is this a good day for you to die?" he taunted.

Gunn didn't answer. Crippled Antelope's words were no different than those of Clay Lassiter or Jace Barker. The red man was just an opponent trying to gain an advantage over his adversary.

With a movement as smooth and as fast as any Gunn had ever seen executed, Crippled Antelope suddenly shifted the tomahawk from his right hand to his left, then threw the tomahawk at Gunn. At the same time, the Sioux's right arm and hand swept smoothly along his hip, the action rivalling Gunn's ability to draw his

Colt. It had happened, literally, in the blink of Gunn's eyes.

The tomahawk arced through the air toward Gunn Gunn's eyes, instinctively, picked up its motion. As Crippled Antelope's right hand swung upward from his leg he had pulled and thrown his knife with a deft underhand motion. The tomahawk sailed by Gunn's head, only inches away. The knife struck home and Gunn felt the flesh of his left thigh separate as the knife buried itself in the muscle tissue. Then Gunn saw something else—something he hadn't counted on. Crippled Antelope was holding a pistol. Where did he get that?

Gunn heard the weapon's discharge. His movement, his trained eyes, every nerve ending in his body worked in unison and all the signals told him that he wasn't the target.

War Eagle's rifle flew from his hand and the warrior slumped forward in his saddle, then tumbled head-down onto the ground. Yes, sure. Crippled Antelope would have to kill War Eagle if he was going to violate the code, otherwise, War Eagle would kill him.

"Gunn!" It was Sinte Galeshka, and he had shouted the name that was the shortest and fastest to say. Gunn looked toward the old chief and saw Sinte Galeshka toss the Colt at him.

William Gunnison's adult life had often hung on fractions of seconds. He was a skilled artisan at gunplay, both feared and respected. Gunn appreciated it, but the most valuable reward he enjoyed was staying alive. The knife Crippled Antelope had thrown could have been fatal. The tomahawk would have been fatal if Crippled Antelope had landed a blow. But the warrior had made a fatal error. He had abandoned the advantage of his own weapons and intruded into Gunn's territory. He had sorely underestimated his opponent. Crippled Antelope wasn't the only person ever to do this. There were many graves filled with the remains of men who had made the same mistake.

Crippled Antelope fired a second time, at almost the same time Gunn caught the Colt which had been tossed to him. What happened then was as natural as breathing to Gunn. In one, fluid motion, he aimed and fired.

Crippled Antelope, his own training, skills and warrior instinct every bit the equal of Gunn's in many ways, knew that he had failed. Even as his finger pressed against the trigger of his pistol for a third time, his eyes had seen the puff of white smoke belch from the Colt's barrel. His brain recorded it and rushed the message to the rest of his body. It melted into his nervous system and turned to fear, then acceptance. The bullet struck, going straight into his heart.

Crippled Antelope's finger eased back. There was no third shot, no more hate, no more revenge.

He was a Lakota warrior and he would die proudly.

# Chapter Twenty-seven

The regimental surgeon treated Gunn's leg while the Indians began leaving the field. Sinte Galeshka sat on the ground beside Gunn as the surgeon cleaned and dressed the wound.

"Where will you go now, Shadow Hand?" Sinte Galeshka asked.

"Who knows?" Gunn said. "There's always another town, another mountain, somewhere. What about you? Where are you going?"

"I will move my people the way the Blue Coats say," Sinte Galeshka answered. "But I will hunt the buffalo and the deer and the hunt will take me to land that the white eyes want and we will fight again someday. Maybe I will fight you, Shadow Hand."

"No," Gunn said. "I won't fight you, Sinte Galeshka. Not ever."

Sinte Galeshka smiled sadly. "Maybe this is true, Shadow Hand. Maybe you will not fight me. But you will kill me."

Gunn watched as Sinte Galeshka walked away and climbed on his horse. He turned and looked back at Gunn, then held up his hand for a moment before joining the other Indians in their long, slow march.

"Now, what the hell you think he meant by that?" Colonel Waddington asked. Waddington and his troops had arrived on the scene shortly after the fight between Gunn and Crippled Antelope.

"If you don't understand it, Colonel, I'm afraid I can't explain it to you," Gunn said. He got up then and walked around a few steps, testing his leg.

"Yes, well, we all owe you a debt of gratitude, even ol' Sinte Galeshka. You've stopped a war."

"I haven't stopped it, Colonel, I just delayed it a bit, that's all."

"I heard you were quite the pessimist, Gunn. I guess this bears that out."

"I'm not a pessimist, I'm a realist. I learned. I don't like what I learned, but I learned it nevertheless. It's still out there, Colonel, like Seth Kinkaid's mountain."

"Mountain? What mountain?"

"Any mountain. Seth told me once that he'd climbed the highest mountain he'd ever seen. He got to the top and he was proud of it, felt strong, powerful. But the mountain felt nothing. It was just there, uncaring if he reached the top or not. He did it again—and again—and again. The mountain is still there, still the same. And Seth? He's wore out."

Waddington looked quizzical, then smiled, then laughed. "And you see the same thing with the Indian problem, is that it?"

Gunn smirked. "That's what I mean, Colonel. The Indian problem? It's not an Indian problem, it's a white man's problem. Finally, we'll deal with it by total destruction."

"I hope not, Gunn, but if it comes to that, the

problem will be eliminated," Waddington said.

"No. The Indian will be eliminated. The problem will still be there. That's what Sinte Galeshka was talking about."

"Yeah," Waddington said. "I guess I see it now."

Gunn saw an ambulance arrive on the field. Lisa Briggs got out of the back and looked toward him, smiling shyly. She made no effort to come to him.

"I heard she had left the fort," Gunn said, nodding his head toward Lisa.

"She wouldn't have it any other way," Waddington replied. "She was bound to be out here while you settled things." He chuckled. "She put quite a store in your ability to take care of things," he said.

"I guess she had more confidence than I had," Gunn said.

"All's well that ends well, I say. By the way, I suppose you realize that you'll be quite the hero once General Hawes files his report. Of course, with enough references to his own contributions to the campaign."

Gunn chuckled. "Is that a fact? And all this time I thought he was going to put me in jail."

"Put you in jail?" Waddington laughed, handing Gunn a cigar and lighting it for him. "Nonsense, you don't put heroes in jail. You parade them around, show them off to senators and congressmen and newspaper reporters from the east. He's already making plans, you know."

"He can make his plans without me," Gunn said. "I'm not about to be paraded around."

"I don't blame you, Gunn, not a bit," Waddington said. "Of course, he could make things awfully uncomfortable for you if you don't go along with him, including the little matter of your hitting him. If he insisted, that could put you in jail for a year, you know."

"A year?"

"I'm afraid so."

"No way. I'll hightail it out of here."

"Then be a fugitive from justice," Waddington said. "There'll be paper on you from St. Louis to San Francisco. You want that?"

"Not particularly, but I don't intend to play hero for him either."

"There's another solution," Waddington offered.

"What's that?"

"If I were to send you off on a job for me you wouldn't be available for all his flag-wavin'. And by the time you got back it would be yesterday's news."

Gunn squinted through his cigar smoke and looked at Waddington.

"What you got in mind, Colonel?"

"The girl, Lisa Briggs," Colonel Waddington said, pointing toward her. "She wants to return to Omaha, and she's asked that I assign you to escort her. Of course, the Army'll pay all the expenses and you can draw per diem. What do you say?"

"That's all? Just take the girl to Omaha?"

"That's all."

Gunn looked at Lisa, at the young, sleek body, the flared hips, the trim ankles. His blood warmed and he felt a faint stirring in his loins. It might be good to spend a few days alone with her. On the other hand, it would be even better to get away, to put this part of his life behind him. He looked toward the distant mountains. They looked cool and inviting. How good it would be to saddle up Esquire and start for them, right now.

"What do you say, Gunn?" Waddington asked. Lisa, probably realizing that Waddington was asking at this very moment, looked at him with silent but pleading eyes.

"Ah, Mister Gunn, there you are!" General Hawes said, coming over to him then. "I've been working on the field report and I want you to hear this." Hawes cleared his throat.

"Not now, General," Gunn said. He looked at Lisa and smiled at her. "I've got to go to Omaha."

Happily, Lisa opened her arms and ran to him, grinding her body against his.

On the other hand, Gunn thought, the mountains could wait.

They would be there.

They would always be there.

# SHELTER
by Paul Ledd

| | |
|---|---|
| #3: CHAIN GANG KILL | (1184, $2.25) |
| #13: COMANCHERO BLOOD | (1208, $2.25) |
| #15: SAVAGE NIGHT | (1272, $2.25) |
| #16: WICHITA GUNMAN | (1299, $2.25) |
| #18: TABOO TERRITORY | (1379, $2.25) |
| #19: THE HARD MEN | (1428, $2.25) |
| #20: SADDLE TRAMP | (1465, $2.25) |
| #21: SHOTGUN SUGAR | (1547, $2.25) |
| #22: FAST-DRAW FILLY | (1612, $2.25) |
| #23: WANTED WOMAN | (1680, $2.25) |
| #24: TONGUE-TIED TEXAN | (1794, $2.25) |
| #25: THE SLAVE QUEEN | (1869, $2.25) |
| #26: TREASURE CHEST | (1955, $2.25) |

*Available wherever paperbacks are sold, or order direct from the Publisher. Send cover price plus 50¢ per copy for mailing and handling to Zebra Books, Dept. 1978, 475 Park Avenue South, New York, N.Y. 10016. Residents of New York, New Jersey and Pennsylvania must include sales tax. DO NOT SEND CASH.*

## WHITE SQUAW
### Zebra's Adult Western Series
by E.J. Hunter

| | |
|---|---|
| #1: SIOUX WILDFIRE | (1205, $2.50) |
| #2: BOOMTOWN BUST | (1286, $2.50) |
| #3: VIRGIN TERRITORY | (1314, $2.50) |
| #4: HOT TEXAS TAIL | (1359, $2.50) |
| #5: BUCKSKIN BOMBSHELL | (1410, $2.50) |
| #6: DAKOTA SQUEEZE | (1479, $2.50) |
| #7: ABILENE TIGHT SPOT | (1562, $2.50) |
| #8: HORN OF PLENTY | (1649, $2.50) |
| #9: TWIN PEAKS – OR BUST | (1746, $2.50) |
| #10: SOLID AS A ROCK | (1831, $2.50) |

*Available wherever paperbacks are sold, or order direct from the Publisher. Send cover price plus 50¢ per copy for mailing and handling to Zebra Books, Dept. 1978, 475 Park Avenue South, New York, N.Y. 10016. Residents of New York, New Jersey and Pennsylvania must include sales tax. DO NOT SEND CASH.*

# TALES OF THE OLD WEST

**SPIRIT WARRIOR** (1795, $2.50)
by G. Clifton Wisler
The only settler to survive the savage indian attack was a little boy. Although raised as a red man, every man was his enemy when the two worlds clashed—but he vowed no man would be his equal.

**IRON HEART** (1736, $2.25)
by Walt Denver
Orphaned by an indian raid, Ben vowed he'd never rest until he'd brought death to the Arapahoes. And it wasn't long before they came to fear the rider of vengeance they called . . . Iron Heart.

**WEST OF THE CIMARRON** (1681, $2.50)
by G. Clifton Wisler
Eric didn't have a chance revenging his father's death against the Dunstan gang until a stranger with a fast draw and a dark past arrived from West of the Cimarron.

**BIG HORN GUNFIGHTER** (1975, $2.50)
by Robert Kamman
Quinta worked for both sides of the law, and he left a trail of graves from old Mexico to Wyoming to prove it. His partner cut and run, so Quinta took the law into his own hands. Because the only law that mattered to a gunfighter was measured in calibers.

**BLOOD TRAIL SOUTH** (1349, $2.25)
by Walt Denver
John Rustin was left for dead, his wife and son butchered by six hard-cases. Five years later, someone with cold eyes and hot lead pursued those six murdering coyotes. Was it a lawman—or John Rustin, himself?

*Available wherever paperbacks are sold, or order direct from the Publisher. Send cover price plus 50¢ per copy for mailing and handling to Zebra Books, Dept. 1978, 475 Park Avenue South, New York, N.Y. 10016. Residents of New York, New Jersey and Pennsylvania must include sales tax. DO NOT SEND CASH.*

# THE UNTAMED WEST
## brought to you by Zebra Books

**THE LAST MOUNTAIN MAN** (1480, $2.25)
by William W. Johnstone
He rode out West looking for the men who murdered his father and brother. When an old mountain man taught him how to kill a man a hundred different ways from Sunday, he knew he'd make sure they all remembered . . . THE LAST MOUNTAIN MAN.

**SAN LOMAH SHOOTOUT** (1853, $2.50)
by Doyle Trent
Jim Kinslow didn't even own a gun, but a group of hardcases tried to turn him into buzzard meat. There was only one way to find out why anybody would want to stretch his hide out to dry, and that was to strap on a borrowed six-gun and ride to death or glory.

**TOMBSTONE LODE** (1915, $2.95)
by Doyle Trent
When the Josey mine caved in on Buckshot Dobbs, he left behind a rich vein of Colorado gold — but no will. James Alexander, hired to investigate Buckshot's self-proclaimed blood relations learns too soon that he has one more chance to solve the mystery and save his skin or become another victim of TOMBSTONE LODE.

**GALLOWS RIDERS** (1934, $2.50)
by Mark K. Roberts
When Stark and his killer-dogs reached Colby, all it took was a little muscle and some well-placed slugs to run roughshod over the small town — until the avenging stranger stepped out of the shadows for one last bloody showdown.

**DEVIL WIRE** (1937, $2.50)
by Cameron Judd
They came by night, striking terror into the hearts of the settlers. The message was clear: Get rid of the devil wire or the land would turn red with fencestringer blood. It was the beginning of a brutal range war.

*Available wherever paperbacks are sold, or order direct from the Publisher. Send cover price plus 50¢ per copy for mailing and handling to Zebra Books, Dept. 1978, 475 Park Avenue South, New York, N.Y. 10016. Residents of New York, New Jersey and Pennsylvania must include sales tax. DO NOT SEND CASH.*